Love In My Town: MM First Time Romance

Van Cole

Published by Van Cole, 2022.

LOVE IN MY TOWN: MM FIRST TIME ROMANCE

First edition. December 14, 2022.

ISBN: 979-8223013709

Written by Van Cole.

Table of Contents

Chapter One...1
Chapter Two...8
Chapter Three 13
Chapter Four 20
Chapter Five 27
Chapter Six 41
Chapter Seven 55
Chapter Eight..66
Chapter Nine..71
Chapter Ten...73
Chapter Eleven...76
Chapter Twelve 84

Love In My Town
MM First Time Romance

By: Van Cole

Foreword

There's a first time for everything...

I should be used to Leah's whims, at this point, strange though they've always been. If my baby sister wants to have a wedding in the middle of nowhere, who am I to tell her 'No'? Even if small town mindsets make me itch. At least the guy running the only bed and breakfast in town, Randall, with his curious nature and kind smile, seems nice enough.

Being the only gay man in a small town isn't easy. Adding to that the past-due rent bills and the stress of managing an empty bed and breakfast, it was a blessing to hear that there would be a large wedding taking place up at the old lodge. I hadn't expected anything of it except being able to actually pay the bills, until I met Mister Tall, Dark, and Handsome. And, unfortunately, straight. Or so I thought.

Love In My Town

Chapter One

Randall Fletcher

Nothing exciting ever happened in this town. Trust me, I would know.

The problem was it just wasn't big enough, or close enough to anything worth a damn. Those travelling through my neck of the woods were on their way to something else; something bigger, or better, or more. Anything that wasn't here.

It's not all bad, I suppose. There were things to do if you knew what to look for, from the small hiking trails through the woods, to fishing in the lake, to manning the only bed and breakfast here, which was where I came in.

The only regular I ever got was Mabel, who was a sweet old lady whom I was pretty sure had been around when dinosaurs still roamed the Earth. She had moved here about three years ago, though I'm still not sure if it counts as moving when you live in a bed and breakfast and have little more than the same six outfits on rotation and a photo album to your name.

She was good company, though, especially on slow days. She liked to sit in the little reading nook by the front desk, people watching and reading her old spy novels.

"Refill, Mabel?" I asked, when I noticed her teapot had stopped steaming and her bag wasn't coloring the water anymore with her third refill.

She smiled up at me, more wrinkles on her face than a bulldog, and patted my hand. "No, thank you, Randall, dear. I should be off."

'Being off' consisted of wandering around the town sticking her nose into everyone's business. That was fine by me – it gave me a chance to clean up the place and she always returned with local gossip and stories, which passed the time well enough.

"I've heard there's going to be a big group coming through here soon," she said conversationally as I packed up her cup, sugar, and empty creamer packets onto a tray.

"Oh?"

"Mm. Phyllis mentioned that Darren was being told to get the old lodge ready for a wedding party."

I paused, then, more out of surprise than anything else. "A wedding?" No one came here for anything, especially something as big a life event as that. "Who on Earth would want to get married here?"

"It's a nice enough place," Mabel said primly, like she did whenever I let my 'Youngblood attitude' show. Her smile didn't change.

"Sure," I agreed. "But still. No one local, I assume."

"Mm."

I finished clearing up her things and hoisted the tray under one arm. The prospect of actually having visitors was almost as foreign as snow in July; it simply didn't happen. My overdue power bills and rooms gathering dust were a testament to that.

"I'll be sure to gather as much information as I can," Mabel said with a mischievous grin I couldn't help but return. I nodded, and brought the tray back to the kitchen, leaving her to be on her way for her daily information gathering sessions.

Life was simple, here, in a refreshing kind of way. My days consisted of getting up, making food for Mabel and myself – I'd had to let my cook go last winter, money was just too tight – and then straightening her room and passing the rest of my day reading or trying to get my shoddy internet connection to negotiate with me long enough to stream a show.

It had been like this for as long as I could remember. My grandmother originally built the bed and breakfast with my grandfather, back when our town was still growing and there were construction workers and contractors to house and feed. But I hadn't seen a customer or new face aside from Mabel in what felt like a century.

There was a little tinkle of the bell above the door, which I assumed was Mabel leaving, so I didn't pause in rinsing out her teapot and cup. But then, another ring came. I sighed, wiping off my hands, and went back to the front.

"Forget something -?" I stopped short. There was a stranger on the other side of the desk. He was tall, with broad shoulders, black hair slicked back and eyes that were so blue they looked fake. He was dressed in a smart business suit like he'd stepped right out of a magazine.

He looked at me, and arched a brow. "Good morning," he greeted. His accent confirmed he wasn't from here; he didn't drawl, had no local twang.

"Morning," I replied, and stepped up to the desk. "Can I help you?"

"I'll be needing a room," the man said.

I'd almost forgotten what that sounded like. "Um. Sure! Yeah, of course. How long for?"

The man sighed. "Let's start with a week," he replied. He looked like he was aware of just how out of place he was. His eyes – Jesus, they were like stained glass, there was no way that was natural, though I couldn't see any ring of contact lens around his irises – looked around us, taking in the dusty shelves behind me, and on the desk, and the sign-in book that had yet to have another signature aside from Mabel's in years.

"Okay," I said. Then; "Are you here for the wedding?"

He looked at me, and his lips twitched into a smile. "That obvious?"

"We don't get a lot of new faces around here."

"I imagine you'll be having a lot more, soon," he said. "I've always tried my best to be early to things."

His smile, slight though it was, was infectious. I held out my hand. "Randall Fletcher," I said. "I own the place."

He blinked at my hand, and then shook it. His grip was firm, and he shook once before he let go, like he had been practicing. "Nathan," he replied. "Nice to meet you."

"You with the bride or groom?" I asked, as I fetched the sign-in sheet and the old credit card terminal, hooking it up. Mabel always paid by check; I wasn't even sure if the thing would work, but this guy didn't seem the type to be carrying cash.

"The bride's my sister," Nathan said.

I nodded. "Well, welcome to Highland Falls."

Nathan hummed, and took the pen I gave him. It was probably dried out. "Thank you, Randall," he replied. He scratched the pen against the sign-in sheet. If he noticed that he was the first name since Mabel's, three years ago, he didn't comment on it. The pen barely managed to write out his first and last name – 'Nathan Monroe' – and the date of entry, and his signature. I took it back from him when he was done.

"It's thirty bucks a night," I told him. "Breakfast is included. We serve it at seven in the dining room." I gestured to my right, through the door with an ornamental frame that was far too fancy for the region. My grandmother had had a taste for finery that suggested old money we didn't have.

Nathan nodded. "I'll be needing your card and I.D.," I added. "Did you drive here? I'll take the license number for your car."

"I took a taxi," Nathan replied. I tried to keep my expression neutral, but another twitch of his lips told me he knew I was surprised. "It was quite expensive," he added, before I could ask. I nodded, unsure of what to say. Nathan's gaze felt like a physical thing, pressure right through my chest, low in my stomach.

"We don't get a lot of visitors," I murmured. He knew that, of course. He handed over his driver's license and credit card without another word, and I swiped it for the first night's fee, which was a non-refundable deposit. The credit card machine took its sweet time trying to connect, but it managed, and coughed up a receipt I tore off and handed back to him once I'd confirmed the name and signature matched. "Alright, Mister Monroe. You'll be in room 3B. The key's in the door already; it's the only copy, so please let me know if you lose it or anything happens to it."

"I will," Nathan promised with a nod. He didn't have anything on him aside from a messenger bag slung over his shoulder. It looked like it was made of real leather, and carried the vague scent of hide. He didn't have another bag, and I couldn't help wondering how he planned to spend a week here, and a fancy event no less, with everything that would fit in a bag that size.

He stood there for a long time, as though expecting me to say something else. I felt heat come to my cheeks, and bit my lower lip. It had been a long time since I'd had to make anything other than polite small-town talk; no one ever came in here, and when Mabel was gossiping, I rarely needed to sneak a word in edge-wise.

Nathan blinked, and squared his shoulders. "Thank you, Randall," he said kindly.

"Do you happen to know how big the wedding party will be?" I asked. The lodge itself wasn't very large, but it had a lot of grounds around it, as well as a nice lawn that could easily sit one hundred people. If I was going to be getting more people, it would be good to know how many I'd need to prepare for.

Nathan's lips pursed in thought, his eyes lifting to the top of the doorway leading to the dining room. "I believe my sister's side of the guest list is rather small," he said thoughtfully. "There's just me and our parents coming, and a couple of her friends. I imagine her future husband's entourage will be a similar size."

It wasn't hard to pick up the edge of disdain in his voice. There was a story there. I bit my tongue and resisted the urge to pry, but couldn't help saying, "I'll make sure his side get put on a separate floor."

Nathan's eyes snapped back to me, brows rising. His smile grew, showing the edges of straight, white teeth. He laughed, sheepishly. "Am I that obvious?"

"New people are easier to read," I replied, answering his smile with one of my own. "You can get away with a lot in a town where no one knows you, and that you can leave behind when you're done with it."

Nathan hummed, and dipped his head in agreement. "Well, perhaps, if you're so inclined, you can let me in on your town's secrets," he said. He even had dimples, good Lord. "I'd hate to leave this place with a bad taste in its mouth."

I knew my blush was dark. I laughed and scratched the back of my neck; my dad always used to say that was how he could tell I was thinking something inappropriate. To his credit, he wasn't wrong. "I'm sure you won't."

Nathan smiled, and nodded again, his fingers wrapping around the strap of his bag as he hefted it a little higher up his shoulder. "I'll see you around," he said, and turned towards the stairs that were by the door to the kitchen. I watched him go, excited at the idea of having guests for the first time in what felt like forever, and to potentially make a friend out of one of them.

A really, really attractive friend. To say this place was lacking in eye candy was an understatement. And being the only gay person around made a jewel like that a rare find, even though he oozed the classic straight businessman vibe.

I couldn't stop smiling as I finished cleaning Mabel's tea away, and then her reading nook. I went to her room first to straighten everything out. She was a clean woman, and fixing up her room took minimal effort. She would need to use the laundry soon, which I usually just threw in with my own.

I spent the rest of the day cleaning up some other rooms, ears pricked for the ringing of the front door bell signaling another guest.

Even though Nathan said he was early, it was always good to be prepared.

Chapter Two

Nathan Monroe

Highland Falls was the kind of place that didn't even show up on the map. The nearest point of interest was the lodge that Leah had, for some Godforsaken reason, chosen as the place she wanted to get married. Probably because it was cheap, and remote, and gave her the impression of being in nature. Even my taxi driver had seemed surprised when I'd told him to drive me here.

It was a nice enough place. Quaint, I suppose, if I had to put a word to it. All the houses were single-story and there were maybe three restaurants and a gas station to its name. It lay at the base of a small range of mountains, covered in a thick pelt of deep, dark green, and had a welcoming humid chill that made it feel comfortable despite the overcast sky and constant breeze.

It wasn't New York. I prefer the city, when all's said and done. Small towns are full of busybodies, desperately trying to find meaning in their lives by seeking out and gossiping about the secrets of others.

I went into my room, shutting and locking the door behind me. The decoration inside reminded me of my grandmother's house; there were flowers patterned everywhere, from the walls to the bedspread to the carpet, so much that I was surprised the whole place didn't reek of them. It was a single room, with a bed that looked large and comfortable, and a small writing desk with a cheap office chair, and large windows that provided me a view of the forest at the back of the bed and breakfast.

There wasn't a phone in the room, but this wasn't a hotel, so I suppose that shouldn't have surprised me. The guy at the front desk, Randall, seemed available enough and would probably be able to get me whatever I needed. I had my cell phone, so it wasn't like I was going to need a landline.

As though summoned, waiting for its cue, my phone rang. I set my bag down and pulled it out, sighing as Leah's name and photo showed up on screen. I answered and set her on speaker, the phone on the desk, while I started unpacking the few changes of clothes I had brought. "Hey."

"Hi!" Leah answered, chipper as always. It was like she'd been walking on Cloud Nine since getting engaged. Or even further back, since meeting Josh. As Leah's older brother it fell to me, traditionally, to make sure this guy was a good one and wasn't going to screw her over and break her heart, which was difficult to do when I lived in New York City and she was still in Denver, where my folks lived and where she had met Josh. "Did you make it to Highland Falls yet?"

"Just arrived," I told her. My laptop had turned itself on at some point in transit, and was running hot as the fan tried to cool the machine down. I took it out and opened it on the desk so that I could force it to go back to sleep. Stupid thing needed replacing, it required updates pretty much every day now and wasn't long for this world.

"What do you think?"

"Seems nice enough," I replied. Mom always said I should be more diplomatic, especially around Leah, who was excitable and easily affected by negativity. That wasn't her fault, she was the kind of person who wanted everyone to be happy, to fix things when they weren't going well, and truthfully, I could be better about that. "The bed and breakfast is...quaint. Feels like it's been here a while."

"I loved it when I went," Leah sighed. "You should go check out the lodge, it's absolutely beautiful!"

I sighed. The time difference wasn't too large, we were only an hour behind from New York here, just past the border of Central Standard Time, but travelling was exhausting. Between the late flight into Chattanooga and then the drive out West, it had been a long night.

"Did you need anything?" I asked, once the very short task of unpacking was completed. There was a tiny closet in the room, where I was able to unroll and hang my suit for the wedding. It was a wrinkled mess but that was one of the reasons I had come early, so that I could hang it and press it so that it would recover and be serviceable. Mom would have a conniption fit if she saw it now.

"Just wanted to make sure you'd gotten in okay," Leah said, "and that, you know... You were doing okay."

I knew what she was talking about. "I'm fine," I replied, hoping that there was enough warning in my voice that she didn't pry. Her well-meaning 'need to fix everything' behavior often made her put her foot in her mouth. "When are you and Josh headed in?"

"Day after tomorrow," she said. If she was upset at me snapping at her, she didn't show it. "I think mom and dad and everyone else are coming in the day after. There's so much to do and so little time!"

"It would be easier if you had chosen a place used to things like this," I couldn't help but say.

She laughed. "But then I don't get to put you out of your comfort zone!" she teased. I rolled my eyes. "Alright, I have to go. Do you think you could do me a favor and check out the lodge? The guy Josh hired said it would be ready in time but I would feel better knowing you'd taken a look at it too."

"Sure," I said. It wasn't like there was anything else to do here. I had told my clients that I would be unavailable today except in case of dire emergencies. The only ones who had my direct phone number were ones I trusted not to call unless the world was ending.

"Thanks, Nate, you're the best," she said. "See you soon. Love you!"

"Love you too," I replied. She ended the call, and there was a click and a beep. I pocketed my phone and unfolded the windbreaker I'd brought with me. I'd looked up the forecast before coming here, glad that, while it was cooler than in New York right now, it was due to be humid. There were going to be a lot of storms, though right now Leah's wedding date remained optimistically clear.

Getting up to the lodge was going to be a pain in the ass unless I could source myself a ride. There weren't exactly a dozen taxis lining up to take me where I wanted to go. Just another way New York was superior, in my opinion. This place had the air of someone who went to sleep at five in the afternoon.

I donned my windbreaker and made sure I had my key, before leaving the room and locking it behind me. I went back downstairs. Randall wasn't there, but there was a little old woman sitting in the reading nook by the front. She brightened visibly at seeing me.

"You must be Nathan," she greeted, and waved. I stopped, forcing myself to smile at her. Her dark eyes glittered with the kind of manic glee only the elderly can have when they see someone new to entertain them.

"Word travels fast," I said, assuming Randall had told her about my arrival.

"I looked at the sign-in sheet," the woman told me, like this was a great feat of sleuthing. "It's been so long since it was just me and Randall here. I was worried we had fallen off the face of the Earth!" She laughed.

"Not quite yet," I replied. "Though I daresay you're in danger of tipping."

"Hah! You might be right about that," she said.

"I didn't catch your name?"

"Mabel," she said, and held her hand out, cupping like I was supposed to kiss her ring. I settled for an awkward handshake, and her grip was tight and the shake lasted way too long before she let me go. "I assume you're here for that wedding," she added. She had been reading a book, and now put her bookmark between the pages and settled it neatly on her lap.

"You assume correctly," I said. "I was actually just about to go check the place out. I don't suppose there's any kind of public transport."

"Oh, Heavens, no," Mabel replied, shaking her head. "But I'm sure... Oh! Randall! It's good you're here, dear."

I turned to see Randall emerging from one of the doors leading to the back. His hands were wet and he was wiping them on his blue jeans, his cheeks pink and mouse-brown hair fluffing up in the humidity. He stalled when he saw me, and then Mabel. If her words were to be believed, and from his behavior, it was clearly new to him to have two people to talk to.

"What's up?" he finally rasped, and cleared his throat.

"Nathan here was just talking about going up to the lodge. Why don't you be a dear and drive him up there?"

Randall's brow creased, and I shook my head. "I'm sure he has things to do here, Mabel," I replied. "I don't want to impose."

Randall cleared his throat, flush deepening. "Yeah, I..."

"Oh, nonsense," Mabel said with a dismissive wave of her hand. "I can hold down the fort for a couple of hours. I know how the machine works and I'm sure I can point people to rooms. Are we expecting a horde of your family and friends to descend upon the place in the next few hours?" she asked, and put her eyes on me, a single brow arching.

My lips twitched, amused despite myself. "Not today," I replied.

"Then that settles it. Randall, go take this nice young man up to the lodge so he can have a look around. I won't hear another word about it."

With that, she opened her book again and turned away from us, as though she was our mother and had a say in what we did. I turned to Randall and shrugged. "If you're not too busy, I'd appreciate it," I said. Randall looked back over his shoulder, still unsure, but then he sighed and nodded.

"Sure," he murmured. "Give me a second to change, then we can go."

"Thanks," I said, and for lack of anything else to do, I sat down on the opposite side of the reading nook, with a little table separating me and Mabel. Even from behind her book, her eyes glittered with satisfaction, and I could tell she was smiling.

Chapter Three

Randall

I was not panicking. No, absolutely not panicking at all. Trust Mabel to be the one who immediately zeroed in on the fact that Nathan was a tall, dark stranger and would try to push us together. I didn't know if she knew about my orientation – she probably assumed, or could 'just tell', as some people insisted they could – but it wasn't the first time she had gone after my lack of social life and friend group. She was like a dog with a bone.

I stank of the kitchens, though, and sweat because it was hot as shit back there. I ran to my room, which was the only bedroom on the ground floor, past the kitchens and in a little addition suite that my grandmother had built once she stopped going up. Originally, my family had lived on the top floor, until we started consistently hitting max capacity, meaning she had needed to convert the top floor to another series of rooms, and my grandfather had built the addition for us to live in.

It wasn't fancy by any stretch of the imagination, but it was comfortable and much more modern. I liked keeping it cold in here, it was more incentive for me to get out of bed and greet the day. I stripped in my bedroom and rinsed down in the shower as fast as I could to get the cling of soapy water and sweat off me, and only gave my hair a cursory rubdown with a towel before running back to my room to find clean clothes.

It was cold in here, of course, which just made me want to hurry more. That, and I didn't want to keep Nathan waiting. Especially alone with Mabel, God, the poor guy didn't deserve that. Mabel was nice enough, but she was pushy and curious and didn't know how to let things go.

I needed to do laundry too, damn it. I threw on a clean pair of jeans, shoved my feet into socks and boots, and yanked a t-shirt over my head. It was chilly outside but I was used to it, and didn't bother with anything warmer.

I grabbed my car keys and ran back out. Maybe I startled Nathan, or maybe he had entered shutdown mode to avoid any potential prying questions, but he straightened up and blinked in surprise at my arrival. His lips twitched in amusement.

"Did you run?" he asked, brows rising.

I was glad I could thank the shower for my blush, but I didn't know what to say, so I just nodded and gestured to the front door. He rose and gave Mabel a gracious nod that she returned, like they were two old friends agreeing to catch up later.

I let him lead the way out, and shot Mabel a warning look. She merely grinned.

"You didn't need to rush," Nathan said mildly as we emerged onto the small driveway that led up to the bed and breakfast. It curled around the back of the building, to a parking lot that was, in theory, large enough to house a car for each available room. In reality the lawn was beginning to get overgrown and there were sections that were starting to crack, letting weeds grow through. Fixing or replacing it was more money than I even wanted to think about.

"I wouldn't leave you alone with Mabel for too long," I replied, clicking the key fob for my trunk until the lights flashed, drawing Nathan's attention. The pickup was almost as old as I was, and had once been red, but now it was so dirty and streaked with mud on the outside that the original color was all but lost.

I kept the inside clean, though. Maybe obsessively, but that wasn't harming anyone.

"She is a rather bold personality," Nathan agreed with another of those smiles that brought out his dimples. Christ, he was pretty, and I was going to be stuck in a car with him for almost an hour, one way. Trying to keep conversation with anyone was a rusty skill for me, and the chances of saying something stupid or weird was high.

I just had to keep it together. Talk about the wedding and the lodge and that was it. I could be chill for a couple of hours. Probably.

"She is," I said. "She likes to know everyone's business. If she bothers you..."

"She didn't," Nathan said, quick to assure me, and shook his head. He smiled. "I'm used to it. My mother is the same way."

That was the kind of thing that could lead to a conversation where I said something really stupid, so I bit my tongue. We got in the truck and I winced at the loud creak of the suspension; another tune-up and series of parts that were in dire need of replacement that I simply couldn't afford. But the old girl rumbled to life readily enough, and I pulled us out of the parking lot and onto the single-lane road that led up to the lodge in the mountains.

There was no radio signal to speak of, so the drive was silent, except for the rumble of the engine and the occasional complaining creak when we hit a bump or pothole. Nathan seemed fine with that; he sat like a robot, hands just above each knee, feet shoulder-width apart, posture perfectly straight and eyes staring straight ahead. This close to him I was too aware of my own slouching, and nervous drumming of my fingers on the steering wheel, and how loud my heartbeat was.

When he finally spoke, we were ten minutes in and I almost jumped out of my damn skin; "You seem agitated."

I sucked in a breath and forced my fingers to untighten from the steering wheel. "Agitated?"

"Mm. I know it's an inconvenience, and I can't imagine you're comfortable leaving your business unattended. I appreciate you doing this."

Oh. Of course. I let out the breath I was holding and forced a smile. "It's really no trouble," I said, and winced internally, wondering if I sounded like every small-town person in the Goddamn world. "I mean, it was either this or walk, and one of the benefits of having an empty business is not having a lot to do."

Nathan hummed. "Hopefully that'll change soon," he said mildly. "If only for a short time."

"Hey, business is business."

Nathan's lips twitched. "I agree."

I was glad that I had to pay attention to the road, so I couldn't make a fool of myself by admiring how his smile changed his entire face, how emotive his eyes were, how they shone despite the lack of sunlight. How his hair, in the humidity, was less severely slicked back now, and tiny strands curled around the nape of his neck and plastered to the sides of his face.

"What do you do for a living?" I asked. His job was safe to talk about too.

"Find thieves," Nathan replied. I hadn't expected that answer, at all.

I frowned. "So you're a cop?"

Nathan laughed. That was the first time I'd heard him really laugh, more than a small huff of amusement. His body relaxed with it, head tilting back. He was tall, hair almost brushing the top of the truck.

"No, I'm not a cop," he said. The laugh ended but his smile lingered, so warm and amused that it made my stomach feel oddly heavy again. "I go to companies when asked to and investigate their financial records, if someone thinks that an employee is embezzling funds."

Oh. "That sounds... interesting," I settled on. "How do you do that?"

"It's fairly obvious once you know what you're looking for," Nathan said. "Checks written to people or businesses that don't exist, large consistent withdrawals, altered checks and balances for contractors, so on."

"So you travel a lot?"

"Sometimes I go there, sometimes they send me their records. Depends how much of a pain in the ass their system is."

I bit the inside of my lower lip, nodding absently. We were getting to the foot of the mountain now, and the path was difficult to navigate at best, even for a native. Trees had a habit of falling all over the place, and if it rained too hard then undergrowth could pile up in the side banks and flood the road out. Not to mention any wildlife that might be in the way. I slowed the truck and shifted the gear down, preparing to have to listen to her whining and grunting her way up the hill.

Nathan looked out his side window, which had the view. He sighed. "It really is quite pretty out here," he noted.

"I think so," I replied.

"Have you lived here your whole life?"

"Yeah," I said, making the first turn. For a moment, the view was obstructed by more trees, so Nathan turned to look at me, and it was distracting. I was glad the road gave me an excuse not to meet those too-blue eyes. "Grandparents built the bed and breakfast, then when they retired my parents took over, and now it's just me."

"I see," Nathan murmured. "I imagine it gets quite..."

He trailed off, and I grinned. "You can say 'boring', it's okay."

"I didn't want to presume."

"Well, you're not wrong," I sighed. "You can probably tell we don't get a lot of visitors here, which makes something like running a hotel pretty much redundant. I've considered selling it to a developer and cutting my losses more than once, but I honestly don't know where I'd go or what I'd do with myself."

"I'm sure you'd land on your feet, with that kind of experience," Nathan said. It was hard to tell if he was trying to be reassuring, or flippant, without looking at his face. But I dared not take my eyes from the road. "I can personally recommend New York, if you have the headspace for it."

"You live in the City?" I asked.

He nodded, and turned to look out again as the trees cleared, affording him another view of the forest and town below. The only buildings that were visible was my bed and breakfast, the slate gray roof easily recognizable to me, and the gas station half a mile down the road. The houses and main street weren't visible for the angle of the trees.

"How long have you lived there?" I pressed, when the silence started to grow uncomfortable again.

"Since I graduated college," Nathan replied. "So, almost a decade I guess."

I huffed. "So you must hate it there."

He laughed again, softer this time, not nearly as dramatic, but it made the air in the truck feel warm. Christ, this was ridiculous, I hadn't felt this flustered around another person since my high school crush; which, as you'd probably guess, was entirely one-sided and absolutely never to be spoken of in a town this small.

"The city never sleeps," Nathan said, voice gentle with affection.

The conversation died again. It was risky to keep talking to him; inevitably I would eventually put my foot in my mouth and say something stupid. Mabel was the only one who I was used to talking to these days and most of the time it was just listening to her dish the dirt on the other residents. But Nathan had a nice voice, it was low and smooth, and I wanted to keep making him smile, and laugh. He looked so much less imposing when he smiled.

"So," Nathan said, saving me from trying to think of something safe to talk about, "tell me about this lodge."

I nodded. "It's owned by this guy, Darren," I told him. "His dad built it, he's still alive but Darren maintains it and I know he's cleaning it up for your sister's wedding. It's pretty and it's got a gorgeous view from the top of the mountain, and some lawn around it where I imagine she'll be having the ceremony."

"Weather permitting," Nathan said, nodding to the overcast sky.

I smiled. "Yeah, she picked one of the less popular times of year to come." Not that any other time of year was particularly popular, not for anyone staying longer than it took to have a nice hike through the woods.

If Nathan had a similar thought, he didn't voice it. "I'm sure it's lovely," he said politely. Then, he sighed. "I'll be honest with you, Randall; I'm not sure why she picked this place either. I'm very curious, once I get there, to see if I understand."

"I'll be happy to give you the tour," I promised. "We're almost there. And we can stay as long as you need."

"You're not worried about Mabel holding down the fort?" Nathan teased.

The reminder did, admittedly, cause a small flicker of unease, but Mabel hadn't lied – she knew how to work the card machine and knew enough about the entry process and how I ran things to be capable enough, should someone else show up. But I worried more about things she wouldn't be able to handle, like a fire in the kitchen or a burst pipe or some other disaster. I'd been lax about keeping up with maintenance on the place, though that wasn't by choice, and it would be just my luck to have the entire building collapse around my ears the second I had guests.

"I think she'll be okay," is what I ended up saying.

Nathan hummed. "I'm sure it'll be fine," he replied. I could tell he was trying to be reassuring, which was sweet of him. My fingers flexed and curled around the steering wheel and I pressed my lips together.

"It's coming up now," I murmured.

Chapter Four

Nathan

Okay, I could see where Leah was coming from. When Randall made the final turn and I was able to see the lodge, I gasped out loud.

It really was beautiful. It looked like it had been built straight out of a magazine, the kinds that boasted luxurious retreats in the middle of nature. It was a large building made entirely of thick wooden logs stacked on each other like planks, the roof was thick thatched straw. There was a border of semi-large stones around the edge of it laden with moss, and vines creeping up one of the visible sides of it, surrounding a brightly painted blue door.

There were wind chimes hanging on either side of the door, framing it, and a chimney with a weathervane in the shape of a rearing horse. Near the lodge was a gigantic pond, similarly decorated with moss-covered stones and bright flowers.

I could only see the edges of the lawn that Randall had mentioned. The road turned into gravel a few feet from the front of the lodge, and Randall drove up to it and killed the engine. Immediately, the sounds of birds and the chitter of smaller rodents in the forest around us seeped into the car.

"Here we are," he said, and opened the door. I followed suit, wincing internally at the loud creak of the door that momentarily silenced the wildlife around us. We closed the doors and Randall circled the front of the vehicle to stand beside me. "Doesn't look like Darren's here, so we have the place to ourselves."

I smiled, and held my hand out. "After you."

Randall nodded, his cheeks red, eyes downcast. He walked up to the front door and, from beneath the welcome mat, he pulled out a large ornate metal key. He fit it into the lock and opened the door, turning on the lights.

It looked much larger on the inside than even its sprawling exterior had suggested. The first room was huge and open, wood paneling on the walls gleaming dully in the light of the soft orange bulbs set into the ceiling. There was a lounging area with thickly padded chairs made of brown animal hide, and a large old wooden rocking chair in the corner. The fireplace was lined with black slate, and there was a carpet on the floor patterned in brown and green that made it look like we would step right onto the forest floor if we touched it.

Randall went to the first door on the left and opened it, turning on the light in that room. "Here's the first bedroom," he said. Inside it looked like a standard hunting lodge themed hotel. The frame of the bed was metal, the sheets and duvet looked thick and soft to the touch. There was another rocking chair in the corner and another fireplace, and a window that looked back out to the truck and the road leading in. The next room he showed me was the same, as was the third bedroom. There was a kitchen area tucked into the back of the main room, little more than counter space built into the back wall, and a woodfire stove, and a small fridge. The floor was linoleum here, and our shoes clicked on it when we walked over. There were two more bedrooms and then what appeared to be a study. In this room were hunting trophies, various taxidermized animal heads on the wall, and positioned on the shelves amidst books. There was a gigantic pair of leather armchairs in the middle of the room, on a carpet, around a third fireplace, and a small cabinet that, through the glass front, I could see held a hoard of bottles of dark liquor.

I whistled lowly, impressed despite myself. It wouldn't be large enough to house all of the guests, but if Leah and Josh wanted to stay up here on their own, they would be able to, and our parents, and some of Josh's entourage. They tended to get overzealous when alcohol was involved and I didn't know how everyone planned on driving back down to the bed and breakfast.

I resisted the urge to say so, for Randall's sake. He didn't need to be worried about potentially losing income. I decided, then, that I would persuade as many people as possible to check in to the bed and breakfast, so that even if they didn't use the rooms, he would be able to charge them. I knew Josh's friends were fairly thrifty, and the lodge was a flat rental that our parents were paying for, so it wasn't like they would lose money if they crashed here on the wedding night.

Leah would probably make them go home, though, for the sake of some privacy with her new husband.

We left the lodge and Randall turned off all the lights and locked the building, placing the key back beneath the mat. Then, he led the way around the lodge, so that I could see the lawn. My eyes widened at the view – it was beautiful, he hadn't been lying. Forest and mountains stretched out as far as the eye could see, in every direction. Even the overcast sky couldn't dampen the natural beauty of the place.

I whistled softly, and nodded. "I can see why she chose this place," I said quietly.

Randall smiled widely. "I used to come up here all the time when I was younger," he said. "It was the hangout spot for high schoolers back in the day. Probably still is, though our demographic is older these days."

Yes, this didn't seem like the kind of town that the young gravitated towards. It was the kind of place coming of age movies were set in when the protagonist wanted to leave everything behind and break out into the big wide world.

The lawn was very large, and would easily seat the entire wedding party and guests. "I can see why," I replied after a moment. Even though I loved living in New York, and the hustle and bustle of everyday life, there was an overwhelming sense of peace here, like time ground to a halt and ceased to have any meaning. It was a bubble of quiet solitude, content with its own existence. I found myself relaxing as well, listening to the sounds of the forest around us, and feeling the gentle breeze on my face.

"There are hiking trails around here too," Randall said after a moment, pointing back the way we'd come. "You can't drive any farther, but there's a trail that goes right to the peak, and there's a small lake and that's where the river starts."

He paused, and asked; "Do you want to see it?"

"Yes," I found myself saying, and meaning it. "I would like that very much."

Randall's answering smile was so wide, a boyish grin that lit up his whole face. "Cool!" he said, rubbing his hands together, and then scratching at the back of his neck. "This way."

He turned, and started back towards the truck. I followed behind, able to keep pace with a more leisurely stride. Randall wasn't that much shorter than me, but he took small strides and more quickly, like he was used to having to be careful where he walked.

True to his word, there was a small break between a set of trees, and a path that looked well-travelled. He started towards it. "A lot of the wildlife here used to be okay around people," he said, "but, you know, with people hiking up here less and less, they've gotten a bit more feral. We might see some deer or squirrels and birds but that's about it."

"No lions and tigers and bears?" I teased.

Randall's cheeks darkened, and he laughed. "No, not that I know of," he replied. He sounded nervous.

I tilted my head to one side as we fell into step together. Despite his normal quick gait, he synced his steps to mine. His fingers kept wringing together nervously in front of him, his head was bowed. "We don't have to do this if you want to go back," I suggested. If nothing else, then with the overcast sky, the sun setting would have a faster effect than if it was a clear day.

Randall looked up at me, frowning. "No, really, I'm fine," he insisted. He was so charmingly earnest.

I smiled, and nodded down to his hands. "You seem antsy."

"Oh." His cheeks darkened to a deep red, and he scratched the back of his neck and shook his head. "No, I'm sorry, really... I mean, I'm not all that concerned about the hotel. This is a nice change of pace; I don't get out much."

I tilted my head to one side. "It's natural to be invested in your business," I told him. "And to feel protective over it."

"I'm fine, really."

Genuine or not, he seemed determined to cling to the sentiment. I nodded. "I won't argue with you," I said. "But I mean it, really, if you want to go back, we can. I can see the lodge another time when you have more time to prepare for a longer outing."

Randall laughed, somewhat bitterly. "Sounds like I'm going to be busy for a while."

I smiled. "That's a good thing, isn't it?"

"Of course."

There was something I was missing, that much was clear. Which was frustrating, but Randall didn't owe me his life story, and it was rare I cared enough to listen even if he had decided to spill it. Which was... novel. To find I did want to know. That I cared about his comfort.

But that was natural. He was being very accommodating at his personal expense. It was normal to care about the mental and financial wellbeing of friends, and I suppose at this point I did already consider us friendly. We barely knew each other, and after I went home would probably never speak again, but Randall radiated the same kind of welcoming peacefulness of the forest around us. If given the chance, I imagined he could be a very calming influence on people.

I was willing to let it go, but he, apparently, wasn't. "I'm sorry," he said. We halted together and I turned to face him. He couldn't meet my eyes. "I guess I'm just surprised. And I want to make a good impression, on behalf of..." He trailed off, and gestured behind us, down the road and to the town as a whole. "Word of mouth is a powerful thing."

"I'm very pleased with what I've seen so far," I assured him. He smiled, shyly. "You don't have to work so hard, Randall."

He winced. "Force of habit, I suppose," he muttered sullenly. Before I could reply, he sucked in a breath and rolled his shoulders. "Don't mind me. Seriously. I'm fine, and this is fun. Long overdue, in my opinion. Shall we?"

I nodded, and let him have some space as we continued up the path. It was clear he was still on edge, for a reason I couldn't fathom. I sighed, internally, and said; "I understand what it's like to want to please people."

Randall hummed. "I guess it's a good thing I don't have many people in my life to please." He swallowed, and scratched the back of his neck. Maybe that was a nervous habit of his. "But I can't imagine it's that hard for you? Big city crime stopper."

I laughed. "I suppose."

He paused. "I don't want to pry."

"But you're curious."

He blushed darkly, but didn't deny it.

I smiled at him. "It's not as exciting as you think it is, I promise. Rather mundane."

"Oh, come on." He rolled his eyes, and I was glad to see that the teasing was helping him relax. His shoulders lowered and he moved a little less stiffly. "You have to know saying shit like that just builds up the drama. You know all I do is sit around listening to Mabel tell me everyone's business?"

"Maybe I'll tell her, then," I said. "I'm sure she would make it much more interesting."

Randall grinned, and rolled his eyes again. The path suddenly became very steep, and more rock than dirt. Randall took the lead and I made sure to place my feet where he did, wary of accidentally missing a step and falling on my ass.

We were both breathless by the time we reached the top. I wiped sweat from my forehead and took off my windbreaker, wrapping it around my waist. Randall continued along a much narrower path, and I could hear the nearby babble of a small stream. The humidity was sweltering and it was far too hot to be comfortable, making our clothes cling together and chafe uncomfortably.

"Here," Randall said, and pushed a branch aside, revealing the top of the path. It wasn't as decorated as the pond by the lodge, and there wasn't as clear of a view, but it was a small, pretty little alcove in the middle of nowhere.

"It's pretty," I said, as Randall carefully let the branch swing back into place, to avoid hitting us both.

"Yeah," Randall agreed with a nod. His hair was flat to his head from sweat, and he pushed it away, making it stick up like a porcupine. "This is where the river first comes above the ground, and goes all the way down to the falls, which, I'm sure you can guess, is how the town got its name."

I nodded. Without the windbreaker, my arms were exposed to the air, and the humidity and sweat was making it uncomfortable. And probably getting bitten to all Hell. Bugs loved biting me.

"We should head back," Randall said, his eyes on the small patch of sky visible between the break in the trees. "It'll storm soon."

"Sure."

Chapter Five

Randall

It did storm. It actually hit us before we were even halfway back, and by the time we got to the truck, our shoes were covered in mud, our legs coated almost up to our knees, and we were both soaked through. It was a veritable downpour, and cold as shit, and I prayed that my truck's heating would be up to the task of warming us up once we got back.

I ran around the side and unlocked the driver's side door, crawling in to unlock Nathan's side so he could get into the truck. He practically threw himself in and slammed the door behind him, breathing hard. He pushed his wet hair back from his face and shivered, unwrapping his windbreaker and covering his chest with it.

I closed my door and started the truck – or I tried to. It chittered and coughed, and a small amount of black smoke came out the tailpipe, but it didn't start. I frowned, and tried again, only to yield the same result.

I slammed my hand on the wheel after the fourth attempt. "Fuck."

Nathan sighed. "Looks like we're staying the night," he said.

I stared out the front windshield towards the lodge, which was blurry and barely visible through the heavy rain. "I guess so," I sighed, and looked at him apologetically. "I'm sorry."

"I should apologize," Nathan replied. "I'm the one who dragged you up here."

I sighed. "Well, I know the fireplace and landline works in there, so at least I can see if Darren can come tow us. Let's go." He nodded, and we ran out of the truck and towards the front porch. I knelt down for the key and unlocked the door and we shouldered our way inside. The electricity held out for lighting, at least, though if it got really bad then that might not remain the case.

Plus, the roads would probably get really bad quickly. I went to the first bedroom, where the landline was, and picked up the receiver. In a town this small, everyone knew everyone's number. Half the population didn't even have cell phones, there was no point.

Darren picked up on the third ring; "Hello?" he asked gruffly.

"Hi, Mister Kinney, it's Randall Fletcher. I'm up at the old lodge with one of the guests for the wedding this weekend, and my truck crapped out on me. I don't suppose you'd be able to come tow us back?"

Darren sighed. "Sorry, son, but I'm not in town right now. And I took the truck with me, got nothin' to haul you with. By the time I come back the roads'll be shit." I sighed, but understood. "Listen, there's food and drink up there, though, and it's guest ready. You should stay the night and if your truck won't start tomorrow, I'll come getcha, sound good?"

"Yes, of course. Thank you," I said, and hung up the phone. I called Mabel, next, at the bed and breakfast. "Mabel, I'm up at the lodge with Nathan, and we're stuck up here, got caught in the storm. Will you be alright until morning?"

"Oh, dear," she laughed, "I'm sure I can make it a day. Stay safe, best of luck to you!"

I nodded, silently glad that she hadn't put up a fuss, and put the receiver back in the cradle.

"From the sound of it, we're staying the night?"

His voice came from right behind me, and so suddenly I jumped in place and whirled around. "Jesus Christ, you scared the shit outta me," I said, taking a step back. Then another, when I realized just how close we were. God, this was like my best dream and worst nightmare combined into one. Being trapped in a storm with a smoking hot stranger was the kind of fantasy featured in pornos and dirty novels, not real life. Certainly not my real life.

Nathan eyed me, lips twitching, but held up a hand in apology. "Sorry," he said, and took a step back. "Leah always said I needed a bell so she knew where I was. I forget."

I nodded. Shake it off. "Darren's not going to be able to come get us until tomorrow," I said. "But he said there's food and drink up here, and, you know, plenty of beds, so...."

"It could certainly be worse," Nathan agreed with a nod. He looked around and behind him from the threshold, one hand on the frame. "If we can get that stove going, or a fire, it'll warm us up faster."

I nodded in agreement, and he stepped back to let me out of the room. I closed the bedroom door, as well as all the other ones so that we kept as much heat in this room as possible, at least until we dried out. "There should be some wood logs... somewhere. Here we go." There were some starter logs stacked up by the kitchen cabinets, as well as a lighter in one of the drawers. I opened the front of the stove and the smoke chute and shoved two logs in, one on top of the other at an angle.

I put the lighter in and flicked it on, glad that it seemed to be relatively new and the flame stretched tall. It was probably one of Darren's that he'd left here during one of his trips to clean the place up. The starter log caught readily enough, and soon flames were licking down it and catching on the other one. I pulled the lighter out and closed the front almost all the way so that it didn't get blown out before it could start generating heat.

A sound caught my attention, and I turned to see Nathan draping his windbreaker over the back of the rocking chair in the corner. He crouched down to take off his shoes and, yeah, I knew I was staring, but it was probably going to be the only chance I got, and Mother Nature had done a great job of soaking his shirt through so it was plastered to his back.

He was skinny, the line of his ribs almost too defined. Mabel would lose her mind if she saw that. Despite his slimness, his shoulders were muscled, his biceps flexed as he moved, and the cut of his shoulder blades was pronounced.

He straightened, and turned, and I hurriedly averted my gaze and took off my own shoes and socks, feeling my cheeks heating in a way that had nothing to do with the woodstove. I put my shoes underneath the stove and laid my socks on top of the bulb of it so that they would dry as fast as possible.

His shadow fell over me and I looked up to see him holding his socks as well. He nodded to the stove. "Room for more?" I nodded, and moved to one side so he could do the same with his socks. It would smell of old mud and feet by the end, but at least they'd definitely be dry by morning. Nathan sighed, rubbing his hand over his face and through his hair, pushing it back. It was wet enough that it looked like he had product in his hair, still, but I knew once it dried it would be back to a natural look. The idea of this gorgeous man all ruffled with bedhead and sleepy was enough to make my heart stutter in my chest.

Nathan sighed, and put his hands on his hips. "On a scale of one to ten," he began, "how pissed do you think this Darren fellow would be if we drank his booze?"

I laughed. "He's been dry for decades," I replied, shaking my head.

Nathan's bright blue eyes gleamed with a mischievous light. "Is that so?" he asked, and when I nodded again, he clapped a hand on my shoulder. His grip was surprisingly strong, his hand fever warm. "Come on, then, not like we have to drive anywhere."

"I don't think this is making a very good impression," I said, but followed him into the study anyway. The cabinet with all the liquor had glasses on a shelf beneath it. They were dusty, so I took two of them and carried them out to the sink, content to let Nathan choose whatever he wanted. I wasn't much of a drinker myself, and certainly not enough to have a preference – when I drank it was to get numb or get brave.

Which, of course, wasn't the smartest move when trapped overnight with one of the most beautiful men I'd ever seen, whom I was certain was straight and would probably deck me if I made a move, but I also didn't drink because I was smart.

Nathan emerged from the study with three bottles, one in each hand and a third tucked under his arm. "What kind of mixers are we working with?" he asked, nodding to the fridge behind me. I turned and opened it.

"Um, looks like some Coke, some Sprite, and... fruit punch." I shook my head, laughing. "Guess Darren's been taking his kid to work some days."

"All easily replaceable," Nathan noted. "Good. You got a poison of choice?"

"No," I replied. "I don't really indulge all that much."

Nathan blinked at me, and then smiled, lopsided and dimpled and pretty, fucking Hell. "I'll go easy on you, then," he said. Like a Goddamn purring cat. Was he like this with everyone he'd just met? He had seemed so stiff and formal not even this afternoon, and now here he was making jokes and...flirting?

No, he couldn't possibly be flirting. But wasn't that a nice thought.

"Let's start mild," Nathan said, untwisting the top of a bottle. I couldn't see the label, but it smelled like Jack, my dad used to drink that. I got a Coke out of the fridge and split it between the glasses, eyes widening when Nathan went ahead and filled both our glasses to the top, so the ratio was at least half whiskey.

"Are you trying to get me drunk?" I asked, but didn't protest when he handed it to me. Our fingers brushed and I almost dropped the glass, and then held it far too tightly.

He smiled. "You need to relax," he said. "If I didn't know any better I'd say you were one of the people I interview for embezzlement, you're so jittery."

"Maybe you're the problem," I muttered, only half-joking. Still, he laughed. I took a sip and winced at the explosion of whiskey flavor in my mouth, flooding it with saliva. It went straight up the back of my throat and made my nose burn and my eyes water. Nathan merely laughed harder at my reaction.

He went over to the couch and sat down, still perfectly proper, as he had in the car. I sat on the other end of it, for my own sake more than anything else. I knew for a fact that the more I drank, the more affectionate I would get, and I didn't need to be able to touch him when that happened.

He sighed, and took a deep pull from his glass without flinching. After a moment, he stood and went to get the bottle, and another pair of Cokes for us to mix them with. He set them down on the wooden coffee table between us and settled back down with a sigh.

Outside, the storm raged. I had yet to see any lightning, but the distant roll of thunder promised that it would come soon. Nathan's eyes were fixed on the fireplace, and a thousand miles away. I cleared my throat when he took another long drink.

"I guess I'm not the only one that needs to relax."

Nathan's lips twitched, but he didn't otherwise move. His fingers tapped, like a countdown, along the edge of the armrest. "I'm not used to just... being still," he admitted. His eyes flashed my way, but didn't stay for long. "Especially with someone."

I tilted my head.

"I like having things to do," he continued. "And I won't lie to you, Randall, I really prefer the city over farms and forests and shit. Like, it's pretty here, I won't deny that, but it's also full of bugs and you can't get a decent cup of coffee worth a damn and everyone is so... close."

His nose wrinkled with barely concealed disdain. I tried not to take it personally. It's not like he was wrong.

"Well, I mean, I don't think there's anything here to do," I said, gesturing to the room as a whole. "But there's always talking. Or drinking ourselves into oblivion and passing out on the couch."

Nathan's lips twitched, and he sighed into his next mouthful. "Sorry. Leah always says I say shit when I should just shut up."

"I think you and I have that in common," I admitted. He turned to me and tilted his head curiously. "I'm... very aware of my ability to cause offense. And I try not to, but I guess I haven't had a lot of practice."

Nathan nodded, slowly. He slouched a little on the couch and tilted his head back so that he could rest against the back of the couch, and stared up at the ceiling. He rested his drink on the arm of the couch.

"I'm sorry you're stuck here with me instead of home," he murmured, after another moment of silence that wasn't quite uncomfortable, but tense.

I smiled into my drink, and took another big gulp of it. Nothing like a little liquid courage to ease past the tension. "Same here," I replied. "But I guess you'd be away from home either way."

"I find myself very comfortable around you," Nathan said, brow creased like this was a new, confusing revelation to him. The warmth in my stomach wasn't entirely from alcohol, at that quiet confession. It was dangerous to hear him say things like that. But I wanted him to keep saying it; this quiet place with a storm raging outside felt like it didn't belong to the rest of the world. Like there was no one but the two of us.

Dangerous thoughts, fueled by fire and whiskey. Impossible to contain.

"I'm glad," I said.

"It doesn't happen often," Nathan continued. His lashes went low over his bright eyes, and he straightened only long enough to kill what was in his glass. He sat forward, setting it on the table, and poured himself another generous serving of whiskey, topping it off with Coke. "People don't tend to like me. It makes sense – my job is to sniff out rats and that doesn't usually come with making friends. I have a... sense, I guess, for people's secrets. It makes others uncomfortable around me."

I could feel my cheeks heating. What did Nathan sense about me, I wondered? Did he get the impression like Mabel claimed she could?

Would he care? "You're a little weird," I said, hoping it would lighten the mood. It did – his eyes flashed with mirth and his smile brought his dimples back out. "But that's not a bad thing."

Nathan nodded again, lips pressed together. He swallowed, and then put the back of his free wrist to his mouth to stifle a yawn. He shook it off and his smile turned apologetic. "Sorry. Long day."

I nodded. "We can call it a night if you want."

"Nonsense, I'm having a good time."

My brows rose. "Are you?"

"Well... I see the potential for having a good time, and I don't want to miss out," Nathan amended. "You're about to get busy, and as soon as my sister shows up, I'm sure I'm going to be practically glued to her side. So I don't want to go to sleep yet."

That was immensely flattering, and I had no idea what to say to that. I wrapped both hands around my glass and kicked my heels up onto the table, crossing them at the ankles. "So, do you want to talk? Play a drinking game, what?" I asked, grinning.

"Mm, what drinking game?"

"I don't know," I laughed. "You're the one from the big city. I haven't hung out with people, drinking, since high school."

Nathan accepted that with another lopsided grin. "Alright, well there's the classics. Never Have I Ever, Two Truths and a Lie, if there's a deck of cards around here we could play Ring of Fire...."

I winced. "I don't think there are cards," I said. "What was that second one?"

"Well, someone, let's say me, says three things about himself. One of them is a lie. You have to guess which one. If you're right, I drink. If you're wrong, you drink, and then we switch." That seemed simple enough, and at least this way I could control what I revealed to him.

"I'm game," I said. It was novel, and made me feel like a dumb teenager again, cooped up and bored with a handsome stranger, grinning at each other over our cheap cocktails and trying to catch the other one out. I didn't socialize much, even back then, but house parties were the only things to do when I was a kid, and games like this always came up.

Nathan raised his glass in a salute. "I'll start," he said, and tipped his head back, chewing on his lower lip as he thought. "Alright. I'll start you off easy. I have three siblings in total. I got my Bachelor's in forensic accounting from the University of Denver, and... I don't have a driver's license."

I blinked at him, and frowned in thought. His eyes turned to me expectantly. I knew he had one sister, and I couldn't remember him mentioning others, but that didn't mean he didn't have them. He had mentioned... Denver, or Colorado? His job could totally have come from a forensic accounting degree. Having a license struck me as the odd one out, but he did live in New York City. It wasn't impossible that he had made it through college without driving and then never needed one.

"I'm going to go with the siblings thing," I said.

Nathan grinned, and drank. "Yep, just Leah and me," he replied, and nodded to me. "Your turn."

Jesus. Okay. It was hard to think with those crystal blue eyes so focused on me. Despite how much Nathan had drank, he didn't seem hazy or fogged in the slightest. "Um. I had my first kiss when I was nineteen. Never went to college." Both of those were true. Did half-truths count? "For extra money when I was in high school I mowed all the lawns and fetched groceries for people in the town."

Nathan tilted his head, cheek smushed against the couch cushions. His hair was drying now, the stove doing an admirable job of warming the air, and he ran a hand through it, mussing it up. I realized that his hair wasn't as naturally straight as his product made it look. It fell in loose waves around his face and cheeks, highlighting the sharp cheekbones, and the flush on them from the alcohol and the heat. "You can't have been nineteen," he finally murmured.

I blushed, and shook my head. "Drink."

His brows rose, but he obeyed. "Really?" he asked.

"There... weren't a lot of options," I said, regretting now my decision to mention it. I hoped he wouldn't pry. It would be nice to think someone who lived in New York at least knew that gay people existed, and didn't have a problem with them, but we were also going to be stuck in this lodge overnight and I didn't want to do anything that might make him uncomfortable or ruin this new burgeoning friendship between us.

"Was it good at least?" Nathan pried, grinning.

I grimaced, and laughed sheepishly, scratching the back of my neck. "Not really," I said. "Neither of us knew what we were doing, we were drunk, I almost threw up right after."

Nathan's laugh came out hard, like a bark, involuntary and loud. "Oh, man, that sucks, I'm sorry," he said, still laughing.

I shrugged. His laughter was infectious. "Your turn."

"Alright." He blew a strand of hair out of his face, and then tucked it back behind his ear. He lifted his glass up and clinked his teeth against the edge. "I prefer cats over dogs. I've always wanted to go to Europe for, like, a year, doing nothing but sightseeing. I'm divorced."

My eyes widened. "You're too young to be divorced," I argued.

He smiled at me. "Drink."

"Really?" I gasped, but took my drink. I killed the glass with that one, and sat forward to refill it. "Sorry," I added, wincing. "That's a sensitive subject. You don't have to talk about it."

"It's okay," Nathan said. He genuinely sounded unbothered. "My folks and family think it was way more serious than it was. Truth is, she and I just wanted different things. She wanted someone who was more present, and she wanted kids, a family, white picket fence, all that shit." He shook his head. "There's nothing wrong with any of that, it's just not what I want."

"I imagine with your job, it was difficult," I said, for lack of anything else to say. "At least... You know, like you said, you wanted different things. Hard to build a family with someone who's not there all the time."

Nathan's eyes darkened, and he hummed.

"That's not a bad thing," I said quickly. "Like you said, it's just different." He nodded, his eyes on his drink. "Was it recent, then?"

"About six months ago," Nathan replied. "Everyone thinks I should be more upset, or assume I'm more upset than I am." He shrugged. "It was an amicable split. We hadn't done anything like buy a house, shared a bank account, nothing like that. Really it was no more dramatic than having a roommate move out."

"Did you love her?" I asked.

Nathan looked at me.

Open mouth, insert foot.

"Sorry," I murmured, looking down.

"You don't have to keep apologizing for being curious, Randall," Nathan said gently. "I'm the one who brought it up."

"Yeah," I rasped. "So which was the lie?"

"The cat thing," he said, grinning. "I'm not much of a pet person in general but I like cats and dogs."

"I used to have a dog when I was a kid," I said, smiling in fond remembrance of Caramel, so named because of the color of his fur. "He was dumb as a box of rocks, but always waited by the door for me to come home from school. He died when I was sixteen, and we buried him in the backyard."

"I'm sorry," Nathan murmured, eyes soft with sympathy.

"He was old," I said, shrugging. "Older than me."

Nathan whistled lowly. "I'm sure he had a great life, and loved you very much."

Affection, both for Caramel and Nathan's gentle reassurances, curled up like twin snakes in my chest and made it difficult to breathe for a moment. I sucked in a deep breath and bit down hard on my tongue to stop myself doing or saying anything stupid. "My turn, right?"

Nathan nodded.

I sat back on the couch, eyes on my drink as I considered what I could possibly say that wasn't a blatant lie. He already knew I didn't travel, could probably figure out I didn't have friends, and it's not like I could even think of an exciting lie that wasn't obvious. And he had just shared something private with me; I wanted to return the favor.

We were both pretty close to drunk enough that going to bed wasn't out of the ordinary. If he reacted badly then we could just go to separate rooms, have a tense drive back in the morning, and forget the whole thing.

"I...." God, thinking of three anythings, truth or otherwise, was getting difficult. "I was born without my bottom two wisdom teeth, so they only had to remove two. I was a straight-A student. And... I'm gay."

Nathan didn't react, for a moment. For so long I was worried he would react badly. Then, he hummed, and said; "I don't want to offend you, but I'm going to call bullshit on the straight-A thing. I've never known a single person to get straight A's in real life."

I laughed, unable to help it. It escaped me like air from a popped balloon, forced and long. "Uh. Yeah. Yeah, that was the lie," I said, and took a long drink. He let me, in silence, and when I was finished I exhaled again and said, "So you're... I didn't make you uncomfortable, did I?"

"Did you?" Nathan asked, frowning. He seemed genuinely confused by the notion. "For the gay thing? Randall." He laughed. "The stick isn't that far up my ass."

I laughed again. Nervous, scratching the back of my neck, and so weak with relief it made me nauseous. "Sorry. I just. Didn't want to make you feel weird."

"Being gay isn't a disease, Randall," Nathan said, with the kind of forceful tone people have when they've had this argument before. "Who the fuck am I to judge you for that?"

"Well, let's just say I don't make a habit of telling people, for good reason," I muttered, taking another drink.

Nathan sighed through his nose. "I understand," he murmured. "Well, I can sympathize, I guess I should say." He shrugged and finished his second glass, and then held it in front of him, as though the meaning of life could be found in the clinging amber droplets on the side. "May I ask why you told me, then?"

"I... feel comfortable around you, I guess," I said, parroting his words back to him. "And you told me about your divorce."

He nodded, and made a low sound. "I'm glad you're comfortable around me," he said, smiling, his eyes shining with affection when they met mine. Then, he turned away, set his glass on the table, and yawned again. I felt my own jaw tighten with the urge to do the same, but swallowed it back. "I guess two drinks was all I had in me," he said apologetically.

I nodded. "It's late," I said. "I'll stock the stove, just pick a room and I'll make sure the vent is open so you get the heat."

"Thanks, man," Nathan said, clapping me on the shoulder. It felt better, and somehow worse at the same time – clearly he was fine continuing to have physical contact, which was nice, but alcohol made his touch heavy-handed, and lingered far longer than it should have. He pulled away and sluggishly walked over to the nearest bedroom, the one by the back wall and closest to the stove. I smiled to myself as he went inside, turned on the light, and closed the door. The vent was accessible from the outside and I crouched by his door and opened it, so that the wood stove's heat would be able to get into his room.

I went into the opposite one, so that the heat wouldn't have to travel as far. It was on the other side, behind the study. The bed looked comfortable and inviting, and the air was so humid it was falsely warm.

I tugged off my still-damp shirt and jeans, shivering as I clumsily hung them on the handles of the closet, and crawled into bed.

Chapter Six

Nathan

Morning brought with it a painful sharpness behind my eyes, a dull but persistent headache, and a cottonmouth that was so bad my tongue stuck to the roof of my mouth, and it hurt to pull it free. I groaned, rolling onto my stomach, faceplanted to the pillows. There was very little light in the room, the lack of orange behind my eyelids proved that, but I knew for a fact that if I tried to get up I was going to instantly end up regretting it.

Damn it. I wasn't a teenager anymore, and hangovers came with a vengeance these days. That second glass of whiskey had definitely been a mistake.

I heard the door open with a near-soundless creak, after a polite knock. The scent of coffee wafted in and I groaned again, managing to peek from behind my mess of hair to see Randall approaching with a big glass of water, as well as some plain buttered bread. Untoasted, so the smell of melting butter wasn't present to make the nausea worse. He set two pills beside the paper towel on which the bread sat.

"It's aspirin," he murmured, in a low and soothing voice. "Try and eat something too, so it doesn't hurt your stomach."

I pushed myself up to my elbows so that I could reach for the water, first. Three giant gulps helped to cure the dry mouth issue, and I was able to take the pills in the next swallow before starting on the bread. Randall watched with the eyes of a mother hen, no longer nervous, but attentive.

Of course, he ran a bed and breakfast. He was probably used to feeding people in the... "What time is it?" I asked.

"Just past seven," he replied. "I called Darren, he said the roads should be clear, so we just have to test the truck and see if we need him. He's already on his way up to finish preparing the lodge anyway, so." He shrugged. "We have about an hour until he arrives."

I nodded. Thanks to Randall, breakfast was taken care of, and the shower here was water drawn from a well that probably had shitty water pressure, and was little more than a wooden stall in the main front bedroom. I could wait until I got back to the bed and breakfast; showering to change back into dirty clothes seemed counterproductive anyway.

"I appreciate it," I said, nodding to the water and the food. Randall smiled brightly, and nodded once. "You're awfully alert."

"I ate after I passed out for an hour," he replied, laughing. "My dad said it was the best hangover prevention known to man. So I've already suffered through the worst of it." He paused, and winced. "Still going to need to drink a lot of water. Maybe we'll end up swiping some of those juice boxes after all."

I laughed, shoving the last of the first slice of bread into my mouth, and washed it down with the rest of the water. Randall took the glass from me immediately and left to refill it, and I used that opportunity to sit up. I had, apparently, fallen asleep in my shirt, but managed to shed my slacks, which were in a rumbled heap at the foot of the bed. Christ, those were going to feel like shit, putting back on.

Randall returned a minute later with a fresh glass of water and handed it to me. "Drink," he urged. "And eat. You'll feel better."

"You make it a habit to take care of drunks?" I asked, even as I obeyed his order.

He smiled. "I like taking care of my friends," he replied. His voice was quiet, tinged with nervousness. "Kind of comes with the territory."

"It's appreciated," I said, because it was. Randall's eyes brightened with happiness at the praise. He cleared his throat and scratched the back of his neck.

"I'll go straighten my room and then watch for Darren," he said. "Let me know if you need anything. Like I said, we have about an hour, so if you need to sleep a little more I can wake you up later."

I smiled, resisting the urge to make a joke about hotel wake up service. "I'll get up," I promised him. He smiled, and nodded, and left the room, closing the door behind him. I finished the water and bread, already feeling better as the placebo effect from the pills did their job.

Putting my slacks back on was a feat of both determination and personal strength, in my opinion. The clothes were dirty and crusted with mud at the bottom, and the specific kind of cold where they still had the illusion of feeling wet. I shivered as I put them on, shoved my fingers through my hair in an attempt to tame it, which was optimistic, and gathered the paper towel and empty glass of water from the edge of the mattress where I'd left them.

When I entered the main room and closed the door behind me, I saw Randall by the front of the main room, his eyes peering out the window to wait for his friend's approach. He looked over when he saw me, gaze caught by movement, and gave me another warm smile. It was nice to see someone who didn't greet a hungover me with exasperation and annoyance.

"Hey," he said. "How's your head?"

"Better," I replied, nodding. "Thank you."

"The tap water's safe to drink, if you need more," he said. "Or, if you sneak one of the sodas or juice boxes I'll just replace them for Darren."

He'd cleared away the evidence of our indulgence the night before. The only thing remaining that told someone we'd been here were our socks, still on the woodstove, and my windbreaker on the back of the rocking chair.

I had my glass in hand, so I went to the little kitchen area and refilled it with tap water, and drank, more slowly this time, I didn't need to upset my stomach and add vomiting to my list of shit to deal with this morning. The light sensitivity was already going away and my headache had faded to a dull background throb.

I finished my glass, rinsed it out with a small amount of soap and the sponge on the side of the sink, and set it on the metal drying rack on the side of it. I wiped my hands with the paper towel and found the garbage can, tucked under the sink, and threw it away.

Randall was still by the window, eyeing the driveway. I went to the woodstove and gathered our socks, and shoes from beneath it. The shoes still felt a little wet in the toes, but there wasn't much more to be done about that. The stove was only radiating a small amount of heat and I didn't think Randall would want to light a whole log again for the sake of drying them out the last little bit. We wouldn't be here that long.

Randall turned when I approached with his shoes and socks. His eyes dropped, and he smiled, soft with affection. It was nice, to be looked at like that. "Did you get a chance to check the truck?" I asked, though I assumed not, since he was still barefoot.

He shook his head, and leaned against the wall as he bent down to pull on his toasty, crisp socks and damp shoes. "I wanted to make sure you were alright," he said.

It was a quiet confession, and unbearably soft. My chest felt tight, overwhelmed by just how nice it was to be taken care of. "I've woken up with worse," I said. Randall nodded, pressed his lips together, and straightened when he was done putting on his shoes and socks.

"You've also woken up alone," he said. "You didn't, this morning. So why wouldn't I help?"

"You like taking care of your friends," I murmured, echoing what he had said mere moments ago. His cheeks darkened to a delicate sunrise pink, and he nodded, turning away to look out the window. "Randall, I..."

The words died in my throat when he looked at me. In the morning light, his irises held flecks of green amidst the brown, there was a ring of gold around the edge I hadn't been close enough to see before. I cleared my throat and smiled weakly. "I want to make it up to you. Thank you for all this." I gestured around us, to the lodge, to the night we'd spent, to him cleaning up after us.

His cheeks turned darker and he bit his lower lip, smiling sheepishly. "You can promise to go home and tell everyone how great a time you had here, and how pretty it is," he said, and looked away again, out the window. "Maybe more will come."

I hummed in vague agreement, head tilting as I heard the rumble of a large vehicle pulling up to the lodge. Randall straightened, and let the curtain fall. "Excuse me," he rasped, and I stepped back to allow him to pass, only just realizing I had essentially pinned him against the window. He hadn't complained.

He opened the door and I followed him out, watching as the giant Ford pickup that looked more like a black beast than a car pulled up and parked behind Randall's little red truck. A man with graying hair and the beginnings – or leftovers, I thought, remembering Randall said he didn't drink – of a beer gut stepped down from the driver-side door and clapped Randall hard on the back, sending him stumbling.

"Mornin', son!" he greeted cheerfully, despite the early hour. I was no stranger to rising early myself, and I remembered Randall saying breakfast at the hotel would be served about this time, so he probably naturally woke up much earlier, but the man, whom I assumed was Darren, had the energy of a squirrel high on coffee.

"Morning," Randall replied meekly, smiling at him. "Thanks for coming up early."

"Have you tried the truck yet?"

He shook his head, and Darren led the way to it. Randall handed his keys over without a word, and Darren got into the truck to test if it would turn on. I left the lodge, closing the door so no heat escaped, and came to stand beside Randall.

He jumped when he saw me in his periphery, and I smiled. "Sorry," I whispered.

"We really do need to put a bell on you," he muttered, but he didn't sound upset. He folded his arms across his chest, shivering in the cold air. It was chilly; the grass was wet with rain from the storm and our breath misted in front of us. "Darren's a magician when it comes to cars," he said. "If he can't get her going then I'll need to take her to a mechanic."

His voice was quiet, annoyed and heavy with the kind of specific sorrow one had when they knew a large expense they couldn't afford was coming up. I watched him, for a moment, as he left the driver's seat and popped the hood of the truck, bent over to poke around inside.

I pressed my lips together, and said; "I can pay for repairs, if you need them."

Randall's eyes widened, and fixed on me in surprise. He swallowed and said; "That's not necessary."

"Randall, it's my fault you were up here in the first place, it's the least I can do," I replied. He opened his mouth to protest further and I put a hand on his arm, squeezing in reassurance. "Let me do this for you. It's how I take care of my friends."

His mouth shut at that, teeth coming together with a soft click. He wasn't tense under my hand, but he was holding very still like a deer in the headlights. "I don't think it'll be necessary," he said roughly, "but thank you. That's very kind of you."

I smiled at him. His cheeks darkened despite the chill outside, and he looked back at his truck, biting his lower lip harshly. Darren cursed from inside, his voice muffled, and as he turned the key, the engine gave a few warning coughs, a tired rumble, and came to life with a rattling groan. Once it was running it didn't sound terrible, but the amount of effort it had taken to get it going didn't bode well.

Darren left the truck and closed the hood, dusting his hands off with a triumphant grin. "She'll get you down the mountain," he said. He had left the keys in the ignition, the truck still running. "But I'd take her to a shop soon as you can."

"Thanks, Darren," Randall said. Darren nodded, and then his eyes narrowed on me, and dropped to where I was still touching Randall. I let him go immediately, Randall had said he hadn't told a lot of people that he was gay, and I didn't want to cause any trouble for him. I could only imagine what the rumor mill would churn out with the fact that we had spent the night here, even though that had been neither anticipated nor intentional.

Randall cleared his throat, and smiled nervously again. "We'll be off," he said, skirting around the other man. "Tell the family I said 'Hi', I'll see you around."

"See you," he called to our backs. Randall and I got in the truck and Randall circled around, prepared to head back down the mountain.

I shivered, and then straightened. "Wait, my windbreaker's still in here."

Randall nodded and slowed to a halt. I didn't want to have him risk turning the truck off and having to repeat this whole mess, so I left with a promise to return swiftly, and jogged up the little rise to the lodge. The door was open and I could hear Darren rummaging around inside.

I entered and found my windbreaker, taking it from the back of the rocking chair, as Darren emerged from the room I had claimed. I grimaced in apology, and held it up in explanation.

He nodded. "I didn't catch your name."

"Nathan," I replied. "I'm the brother of the bride."

"Ah." His expression cleared with understanding, and he nodded again, folding his arms across his chest. "I see." The way he said that made me feel uneasy, but I had left Randall alone out there, and I didn't want to keep him waiting. He had a business to get back to and I desperately needed a shower.

Not only that, but I just... liked being around him. This place was nosey and small and had little to offer in the way of entertainment, but he was pleasant to be around. Like this haven at the top of the mountain. Like coming home to someone.

Darren huffed. He seemed like the kind of man who was gruff by nature, so I didn't take it personally. "Well," I said, and stepped back, "I'll see you around, I guess."

"Yep," he replied, popping the 'p'. I left the lodge and hurried back to Randall's truck, climbing inside with a sigh.

Something must have shown on my face, because Randall winced, even as he shifted the car back into gear and began driving back down the mountain. "I should have warned you about Darren," he said apologetically. "He's... old-fashioned."

I tilted my head to one side. "Does he know?"

"We have one of those fun 'Don't ask, don't tell' policies," Randall said with false lightness. "He's been an old family friend since before I was born, and he and my dad were really close. War buddies, you know?" I nodded. I did. "But that kind of means I have to let him think certain things." He sighed.

"I'm sorry," I murmured. "I didn't think..."

"It's okay." Randall's smile, though slight, was genuine. "You didn't know."

I frowned. "I think it's bullshit that you feel like you need to hide part of who you are from everyone you know," I said. Randall winced, and pressed his lips together, his eyes fixed determinedly on the road. "I don't judge you for doing it, I know self-acceptance isn't all sunshine and rainbows, even in this day and age, I'm just... angry on your behalf."

Randall hummed. "Well," he said softly, "maybe if I had someone worth coming out for, I would. But I don't."

If he stayed here, he might never. I resisted the urge to say so; he probably already knew that. It might keep him awake at night, how lonely and unhappy he is. Or maybe he didn't give a fuck because not everyone needed someone to be happy. Even when I shared an apartment with Vicky, there were times when coming home to her wasn't as attractive as being on my own. Other people took energy I didn't always have.

Maybe Randall was the same way. He seemed more social than that, but from what I'd seen and he'd told me, he hadn't been able to actually practice it all that much. He would probably need a break from time to time too, and short of 'renting a room' to some man for hire, hidden away on the top floor, there was no way to keep a relationship a secret in a town this small.

I sighed. "That's understandable," I said. His eyes darted to me, briefly, before going back to the road. He pressed his lips together, and they looked tender from how much he was chewing on them.

"Did you eat?" I asked. He blinked, and frowned, and shook his head. "You hungry?"

"Yeah," he admitted. I wanted to ask why he hadn't eaten, then, but resisted; if the answer was something to the effect of that he had given me the only food available, or that he hadn't had time because he was cleaning, then I had no idea how I was going to react. He was so self-sacrificing and kind, it was as foreign to me as all this greenery.

"Well, when we get back, and clean up, let me take you to lunch, or a late breakfast or something, as another 'Thank you,'" I said. He looked at me, eyes wide. "I know my sister's not coming in until tomorrow, neither is anyone else. Or, if you're not willing to leave the bed and breakfast, I'll go get us something."

"I... You..." It was clear that he wasn't used to anyone doing anything like that for him. He swallowed, fingers flexing on the steering wheel. "That's not necessary."

"I know it's not necessary, Randall," I said with a smile. "I want to do something nice for you."

Randall swallowed. "I... I don't know if the truck will take you into town," he said, "and the restaurants here won't be open yet, and getting a taxi would be ridiculous."

Poor guy looked like he was going to have a heart attack. "What if I cooked for you, then?" I offered. "I swear, I'm pretty good. Been having to feed myself for a while."

Randall exhaled heavily. "...Okay," he said weakly.

"Okay," I replied, nodding. I patted him on the shoulder and smiled. He still seemed tense, so I pulled back and put my hands on my knees, shoulders rolling back and settling against the scoop of the seat. Though I hadn't been awake long enough to appreciate or assess the mattress, it felt like it had been a comfortable enough sleep; my shoulders weren't tight and there was a small crick in my neck, but that was probably from not doing anything to adjust the fluffy pillows.

We spent the rest of the ride back in relative silence. It was companionable, both of us too tired to make it tense. When Randall pulled into the parking lot of the hotel and turned off the truck with a wince, we both got out and walked to the front door together.

"Showers, and then I'll make you food," I promised him. He nodded, eyes still wide, like he couldn't believe it, like he had expected me to forget. I smiled, squeezed his shoulder, and walked in through the door.

Mabel was in the reading nook, absorbed in her book, and looked up when we entered. She arched a thin brow. "You boys look like you had a rough night," she noted.

"Well, at least we know now the lodge is habitable," Randall replied. She laughed.

"Always seeing the silver lining."

I smiled, and nodded to Randall. "I'll see you in a minute," I said, and then went upstairs towards my room. I had only brought my key with me, and when I entered the room and set it down, locking it behind me, I checked my cell phone, which was still on the desk.

There were seven missed calls from Leah, and so many text messages that my phone screen was full of them, even the ones that had collapsed into the same message group. I winced, knowing I would be in for it once I managed to answer those messages.

But first things first. Namely, a shower. I was gross with dried sweat and rainwater and mud. I stripped down and put the dirty clothes in a corner. Hopefully Randall would let me use a washing machine here before I left, so that I didn't have to travel back with such dirty clothes.

Besides, I'd only packed two full sets of clothes, one additional shirt, and the suit that was hanging in the closet.

I went into the bathroom and closed the door, turning on the light and rattling little fan. The shower was a stall barely large enough to fit in, but when I turned it on the water sprayed out powerfully, and was hot instantly. I sighed in relief, scrubbing my fingers through my hair and over my neck and face. Randall had stocked the bathroom with travel-sized shampoo, conditioner, and body wash bottles, and there was a small towel hanging from a hook on the other side of the shower, next to the shelf of clean towels. I reached past the curtain and took the hand towel and liberally doused it with body wash.

Scraping off the sweat from the hike, the mud, and the general cling of the outside was a soothing gesture, monotonous. The water was scalding hot and beat down on my shoulders wonderfully. I could easily spend ages in here, watching the water go from murky to clear.

I scrubbed down my arms, chest, and legs, and set the towel down as I lathered shampoo into my hair. It smelled of tea tree oil, a crisp scent that helped with the ache still hanging around behind my eyes. By the end of the shower I felt like an entirely new person.

I got out, towel slung around my waist as I drip-dried, and went back to my phone. I sat on my bed, elbows on my knees, and opened the missed call list first. Most of them were from Leah, one was from my mother, another from my doctor's office confirming an appointment next week. Nothing from clients, thank God.

The messages were from Leah, my mother, and my father. All separate but all saying the same thing: Was I alright? Did I make it there safely? 'Call me when you can'. I was willing to bet the two voicemails said the same thing.

I sighed to myself. It was like when Vicky and I split up they forgot that, before her, I had been taking care of myself perfectly fine for years. I'd met Vicky at one of my client's firms. She'd been tasked to show me around and make sure I had everything I needed to do my job. She was confident and beautiful and kind – well, she still is. It wasn't like she'd died.

I hadn't lied to Randall about why we split up. She wanted kids, and a family, and to settle down with someone outside of the city, probably in a place just like this. She would have loved it here.

Kids weren't for me. I had nothing against them, I just knew with how much I traveled and was away, it wouldn't be fair to bring a child into that, let alone pretend I had any hand in raising them. That was like expecting Santa Claus to raise your kids. I owed it to Vicky to be honest about that, and it turned out that had been a dealbreaker for her.

It was an amicable split, I hadn't lied about that either. At least we had come to that crossroads sooner than later, and didn't have to start all over again with five or more years lost.

But the only people who wanted me to have kids more than Vicky was my mother. I had hoped Leah getting married would turn the attention off me for a while, but alas.

I didn't like dwelling on this. I could be downstairs making food for Randall, or at least getting dressed. I sighed and texted Leah, first, because if she knew I was okay then my parents would find out eventually; "Sorry, went to the lodge and got caught by a storm last night. Had to wait it out, left my phone here. The place is gorgeous and looks ready. See you tomorrow."

That would have to do for now. I checked my email from my phone and saw that no clients had emailed me, either. That was a stroke of luck, maybe all the thieves had decided to take a day off. Or maybe my boss had actually taken my vacation request seriously this time and was having Jimmy handle everything while I was out.

Stranger things had happened. There was a first time for everything.

I rose, and pulled on the pair of jeans I'd packed, as well as a long-sleeved dark blue shirt that would keep me warm if I had to go outside again. I hung up my windbreaker on the back of the door, put on a fresh pair of socks and slid back into my shoes, and went downstairs.

"He's just... so Goddamn nice, Mabel. And now he's offering to pay for fixing the truck and..."

I paused on the steps, just out of sight, frowning. That was Randall's voice.

"Well, dear." Her reply was quieter, and I strained to hear it; "You're not taking advantage of him if he offered. You do a lot of things for me that I know my bill doesn't cover, and you don't complain once. Perhaps he's just trying to do something nice for you."

"Yeah, I know," Randall said, sounding miserable. I frowned. "I just... I feel like I'm taking advantage of him."

"Mm. Perhaps there's another reason you feel that way," she said mildly. Even though I couldn't see either of their faces, I knew what Randall's confused frown sounded like at this point. "This book I'm reading right now – it's very interesting, you should read it when I'm done – the main character is torn because she is attracted to the love interest and feels guilty about it whenever they interact. It's... juicy."

Randall made a choking sound. "I'm... You..." He cleared his throat and coughed. "I don't think that... applies here," he finished weakly.

Mabel huffed. "Dear, I've known you since you were a carpet bug, you don't get to stand there and tell me I don't see what I see." Her voice turned triumphant; I could see Randall now, blushing heavily, scratching the back of his neck. "You're allowed to like attractive people. I'll admit, if I were a few years younger..."

Randall laughed. "You'd tear him to shreds, Mabel," he teased. Then, he sighed. "I don't... I mean, he knows I'm... But he's not. He's divorced. From a woman."

"Yes, because we all know having one slice of pie at a picnic means you can't have any other type of dessert for the rest of your life," Mabel said with false solemnity. Her eyeroll was as audible as Randall's laugh.

"But I won't push you. I'm simply saying that if he wants to do something nice, you don't have to feel guilty just because you're attracted to him. In fact, I'd argue if he's straight, it's nicer? Means he's not doing it to buy his way into your delicates."

Randall laughed again. "You're impossible."

"It's a knack."

That seemed like a good time to make myself known. I carefully prowled back up the stairs, and came back down them, making sure I was overly-loud so that Randall could hear me coming. When I got to the bottom, Mabel was still in her reading nook and Randall was behind the front desk. He smiled warmly at me in greeting.

"You didn't shower?" I asked, pretending to be confused. If he had been talking with Mabel this whole time then he wouldn't have even gotten a chance to.

He flushed, and shook his head. "Needed to catch up on how the fort handled overnight," he said, nodding to Mabel.

"No fires, I assume?" I teased.

His blush darkened, and he nodded.

"Well, that's good to hear. Why don't you go, then, and I'll make us something to eat. Mabel, would you like to join us?"

"Thank you, Nathan, but I already ate."

I smiled at her, and nodded. Truthfully, I only asked to be polite, and was relieved when she declined. Maybe she knew that. Her dark eyes seemed to glitter with smug joy. I turned back to Randall, and he nodded his head quickly, his eyes flashed to the door, nervous, again, about leaving it alone, probably. But he relented and disappeared through the back rooms, and after a moment, I went behind the desk myself.

I opened the door I'd seen him come through when we first met, and saw a kitchen beyond it. Grinning in triumph, I entered the room and shut the door behind me, ready to go through what Randall had in the fridge and make breakfast for us both.

Chapter Seven

Randall

Oh shit, holy crap, shit, shit...

He hadn't... heard, had he?

He wasn't behaving weirdly, and I was sure if Mabel had seen or heard him coming she would have said something. I hadn't heard him coming, but sound traveled through the thin walls and floors in this place, and what if he'd heard our voices before coming down the stairs and...?

Oh God, what if he'd heard me say I was attracted to him? No, he hadn't heard, he couldn't have possibly heard, or he'd have said something. He didn't seem like the kind of person who would spare feelings for the sake of a little white lie. Or what if he planned on doing that over breakfast?

My heart was pounding so heavily I felt sick, as I closed the door to my bedroom, leaned back against it, and tried to get a grip. This was ridiculous. We were both adults. If he had overheard, he would say something, and then we could move past it. Yes, I was attracted to him – I dared anyone with eyes not to be – but he was also nice, and weirdly funny, and I just liked being around him. So I could promise him that my attraction didn't mean anything, and it certainly didn't have to be reciprocated, and just hope he was comfortable with that, and move on.

Assuming, of course, he brought it up at all. Assuming he'd heard, and there was no way to ask without him potentially asking what I was talking about, which meant I would have to actually say it again, to his face.

And he wasn't making it easy, coming down the stairs dressed like some Goddamn boy next door fantasy, hair still damp and fluffy, smiling with those dimples and offering to cook. Jesus Christ. God must truly hate me to torture me this way.

I stripped and showered as quickly as possible, pointedly ignoring my brain whenever it tried to linger on things like the stretch of Nathan's shoulders beneath his shirt, the adorable crease in his brow, the way his hair fell in front of his eyes when he hadn't groomed it back, making the blue look black and giving him a wild look, easily shedding five years off his face.

I didn't let myself think about it, for the sake of my sanity and hot water tank. I got out and toweled off briskly, and threw on another pair of jeans and a t-shirt that I had owned since high school, it sagged at the collar and felt more like old sheets than an actual t-shirt, but it was comfortable.

I left my rooms and smelled... something fantastic. The scent of bacon and butter and salt reached me, an almost physical urge pulling me along, back to the main lobby and then into the kitchens. Nathan was there, flipping over strips of frying bacon with a pair of tongs. His hair was pushed back from his face, curling behind his ears, his brow furrowed in concentration. The oven was on and I could smell baking biscuits, and there was another pan beside the bacon that was going unused at the moment.

He looked up when I entered, and grinned brightly. "About ten more minutes," he said apologetically. He wasn't acting any differently. He hadn't heard what Mabel and I had been talking about. I let out a quiet sigh of relief.

The kitchen doubled as a dining room as well, though the 'dining room' part was just a little table on the other wall with three chairs. My parents and I used to eat here when they still ran the place, away from the guests. Now, with just me and Mabel, we often ate out in the reading nook while she regaled me with tales of everyone else in the town, and we soaked up the sunlight like cats, content with knowing that we had yet another day of mindless indulgence to occupy our time.

I didn't want to eat out in the nook with Mabel, nor did the idea of going into the guest dining room and eating there seem practical, so

I brushed past him and went to the cabinets beside him, taking down two place-sets, and took two sets of utensils from the kitchen drawer. I set our places, and then fetched jam from the fridge, as well as honey, and butter in a small dish. I brought over knives for each of those. Nathan had a glass of water beside the stove.

"Do you want coffee?" I asked.

"That would be great," he replied. The coffee machine was on the other side of him, pinned between the stove and the fridge. I skirted around his back and emptied the filter from the day before, tossing it out, and filled the pot with water from the sink, poured it in over a fresh filter with grounds inside, and pushed the button to let it brew.

I remained in front of it, hyperaware of how close we were standing. If Nathan cared, he didn't say anything, just kept his attention on the bacon. "It's finnicky," I explained anyway. "Gotta watch it."

He nodded. "Do you like your bacon crispy or not?" he asked, gesturing to the pan. Right now the strips were just at the point where someone who preferred them a little floppy would take them off.

"Crispy is good," I said. "Not burned, though."

He nodded again. The oven timer beeped, and he wrapped his hands in a dish towel and opened the oven, peering inside. He took the tray out, revealing a neat dozen fluffy biscuits, gently steaming. Without a word I handed him a bowl, and he carefully scraped each one off and into the bowl, and covered it with the same towel so they remained warm and didn't dry out.

"Eggs?" he asked.

I smiled. "Scrambled is fine. You seem comfortable in the kitchen."

"I like cooking," he replied with a shrug. "Recipes are straightforward, even the complicated ones. It's hard to screw something up when you're told exactly what to do."

And wasn't that relatable as Hell. "I had to learn when I had to let my cook go last year," I told him. "Couldn't afford it anymore. Mabel's never complained but I can't make anything too complicated."

"I'm sure you're more than capable," Nathan replied with a smile. I smiled and turned my attention back to the coffee machine. In my periphery, I watched him crack eggs against the side of the pan one-handed, expertly parting the halves into another small bowl on the counter. He cracked six in total, and whisked them briskly with a fork, adding a splash of milk. Then he heated the pan and poured the mixture into it. Through it all, close as I was, I felt every brush of disturbed air, and could smell the generic shampoo I'd bought for guest bathrooms. He looked comfortable here, at home, and it was gratifying to see him settling in so well.

I startled when I heard the office phone ringing, and sighed. "Be right back," I told him, and left the room to go answer it. "Highland Falls Bed and Breakfast, this is Randall, how can I help you?"

"Morning, Randall!" a female voice greeted, bubbly and chipper. "My name is Leah Monroe. My brother is staying at your hotel. I was wondering if you knew if he was there? He's not answering his cell phone."

"Oh. Yes, of course," I said, swallowing. "I'll go check. Would you like to hold, or shall I have him call you?"

"Just have him call me, if you don't mind. Thanks!" she said, and hung up. I put the phone down and returned to the kitchen.

"Your sister just called," I said. He looked up, and rolled his bright eyes, smiling fondly. "She wants you to call her."

"Probably so she can yell at me for being radio silent last night," he said, and I felt my cheeks heating, remembering why. "I'll go call her. You good to finish up here?"

"Sure," I said. It was just bacon and eggs, both of which were almost ready. He nodded, and smiled, moving past me with a parting squeeze to my shoulder. The place where he touched felt like it was burning, long after he left.

I removed the pan with the eggs from the heat when they were done, carrying them over to our plates, and gave each of us half. Then, the bacon. I took out a third plate and lined it with paper towels, using a spatula to remove the strips and setting them down so the towel would soak up the grease. I carried the plate and bowl of biscuits over to the little table and set them down. The coffee was almost ready, so I took Nathan's water glass, filled it, and carried it over, and set down mugs for the coffee, a carafe, and creamer and sugar packets between our plates.

I did one last sweep to make sure I hadn't missed anything. There was salt and pepper on the table, as well as a small bottle of hot sauce. I made sure the oven and stovetop were turned off, pushed the pans back so they could cool, and took my seat just as the door opened again, revealing Nathan. He didn't look upset, so I guessed that his sister hadn't been too hard on him.

"Still in one piece," I noted. He grinned, and took his seat opposite me.

"Yeah, she wanted to let me know that our parents should be here tonight," he replied with a sigh. "And to give the obligatory 'you had me worried sick' speech."

I smiled. "She loves you," I said, and he nodded. "It's natural to be concerned when a loved one suddenly stops responding."

"Oh, I don't blame her in the slightest," he replied, sectioning off a mouthful of eggs with the side of his fork. "My family considers me a flight risk, considering I moved halfway across the country at the earliest opportunity, and travel so much. I would think they would just be used to the fact that sometimes I can't be reached, but apparently that's not in the cards yet."

I nodded. "What does Leah do for a living?" I asked, as we began to eat.

"She's kind of a half stay-at-home wife. She makes things and sells them online. Paintings, crafts, you name it." I liked the way his voice went soft when he spoke of his sister. Clearly he loved her very much. "She's always been artistic like that."

"I can't wait to meet her," I said, and then realized how that sounded. I blushed, and added hurriedly; "I mean, she seems nice, and I hope she likes it here."

Nathan's smile was small, his gaze gentle. He swallowed, clearing his throat, and set his utensils down. "I wanted to talk to you about something, Randall," he said. "I debated keeping it to myself, but I've always tried to be honest with my friends, and I figure, you know, there was no point not saying anything about it."

I felt my heart immediately leap up into my throat, panic making my hands shake. I set my fork down and pushed them into my lap to hide them, shoulders hunching up. "Okay."

Nathan nodded, and pressed his lips together. He sighed through his nose, and said; "I overheard what you and Mabel were talking about, earlier."

Oh God. If the Earth could open up and swallow me whole, that would be just perfect. My cheeks went hot and a cold knot of dread settled low in my stomach, and in my throat, making it impossible to swallow. "Oh," I croaked. Nathan's gaze was unwavering. I was suddenly very sympathetic to the people he must interview, caught in the act of doing something bad.

Not that I had done anything bad, per se. Being attracted to him wasn't something I could help. And I had no intention of acting on it. "I'm sorry, really. I don't want to make you uncomfortable, and if you're..."

"Randall." He held up his hand to stop my nervous babbling, and smiled. "I'm not upset. It's actually quite flattering." God, just kill me now. "I suppose what concerns me most is that... well, I don't want to hurt you, intentionally or otherwise."

"I know you're straight," I said. "I didn't expect anything to happen."

"...Well..." He bit his lower lip, head tilting just slightly to one side. He seemed stuck for something to say. I wasn't in any position to help him. The silence was so tense I could have cut it with a knife, just begging to be broken, but I had no way of breaking it. The only option seemed to be making a quick and graceless getaway, but there was nowhere for me to go – or him, really. He had no car, he wasn't from here, he didn't know the town. I had to stay here and run the bed and breakfast.

Nathan, eventually, sighed, and shook his head, huffing a sheepish laugh. "I've made you uncomfortable."

"Only because I really don't want to lose you as a friend," I said.

He looked up again. "Really?"

"I'm trying your whole 'let's be honest with each other' thing," I rasped.

He smiled, widely, his cheeks dimpling. They were turning a little pink too, I noticed. I scratched the back of my neck, searching for something else to say. He wasn't calling me a slur or getting angry, wasn't on his feet and ready to beat the living shit out of me, which was more than I could say for the only other person I'd outright confessed my orientation to.

"I don't want to lose you as a friend either, Randall," he said quietly, when the silence turned from tense to unbearable. I didn't want to let myself hope, but that was the thing about hope; I was as helpless to resist it as I was the urge to laugh when Nathan laughed. His infectious smile and kind eyes made my chest feel tight, heart hammering away, nervous butterflies in my stomach. "And I... Well, I won't say I've ever been attracted to a man before, but truthfully, I've rarely been immediately attracted to women, either. I usually have to get to know someone first, and most of the time people don't tend to... get to that point, I guess."

I laughed, awkwardly. "I doubt that," I said. "Have you seen you?"

He grinned, cheeks darkening, and dropped his gaze.

"I don't want to fuck this up," I said, "but I really need you to give me a hint, here, because I'm so anxious I might throw up and I don't want to keep batting a hundred on guys I've liked and then puked on."

He met my gaze again, brow creasing for a moment, before it smoothed in understanding. "Your first kiss was with a guy," he realized, and then nodded. "I don't know why I assumed otherwise, even after you told me you were gay."

"It's an easy assumption to make," I said, shrugging. My fingers kneaded anxiously at my thighs. "But that's not... You didn't answer my question."

He nodded, sighing through his nose. "I know it's kind of an asshole move," he conceded. "But... If you're willing, we could..." He made a vague, aborted gesture with his hand, which gave me absolutely no hints whatsoever. But it was enough to make every muscle in my back tense. Nathan made another frustrated sound, as if annoyed at his own lack of ability to form words.

He nodded to himself, and then stood, pushing his chair back. He circled the table and I scrambled to my feet as well, already panting, heart in my throat. How he managed it, I couldn't say, except one moment we were both standing a foot apart from each other, and the next moment, my shoulders hit the wall, and there was a hand on my cheek and another on my hip, pinning me against it.

His eyes were even brighter and more focused this close, and my hands shook as I clutched at his shirt, at his sides. He smiled, lopsided, sweet, and leaned in until our foreheads touched. Noses brushing. Then, his hand slid from my cheek to just under my chin, tilting my head up, and his lips met mine.

They were soft, and warm, and his kiss was gentle. Tentative, almost, like sampling a new food he'd never tried before. I suppose, in a way, he hadn't. But he didn't pull back. The hand on my hip felt like it was made of liquid heat, piercing straight through my stomach and into my lungs, making me gasp. He took advantage, tilting his head to one side, deepening the kiss with a questioning flick of his tongue.

I closed my eyes because there was no way I wasn't going to lose it completely if I kept them open. I slid my hands to his back, flattening them, urging him closer. He went eagerly, with a rough sound that made every inch of me shiver. He moved his hand from my chin to my hair, spreading his fingers wide to protect my head from hitting the wall. His nails along my scalp made me dizzy, the way his other hand tightened on my hip, then slowly slid up to grip my waist, the way he kissed, assured and hungry, made my knees threaten to buckle.

He pressed closer, until we were touching chest to knee. One of his thighs wormed between mine and yes, shit, that was fantastic. I dragged my nails across his strong shoulders, up into his hair, tightened and twisted them in his thick, wild hair, and the sound he made when I did that went straight to my stomach.

The kiss ended, both of us panting, his mouth red. He met my eyes, questioning, searching, and I barely had time to nod before he was on me again, braver this time, both hands on my hips to keep me still as he arched into me. My shoulders ached from the hard pressure against the wall, and other parts of me were certainly trying to make their need for attention known. But this was – well, it was fucking fantastic. I could taste salt in his mouth, toothpaste, smell his shampoo, and let out a quiet, desperate sound of my own when he dug his nails into my hips hard.

He pushed his thigh more firmly between my legs and I tensed, hissing a breath at the sharp stab of arousal that went right to the backs of my eyes. He stilled immediately, pulling back, his cheeks the same dark red as raw meat, lips bruised and tender, slick with spit. He licked them, panting, and smiled sheepishly.

"Sorry," he murmured.

"Stop fucking apologizing," I rasped.

He laughed, tension melting from him like snow in summer. "Sorry," he said again, and I had to laugh. It was ridiculous and I was giddy.

I swallowed, and slowly unwrapped my fingers from his hair. His lashes went low, head tilting and shoulders rising like he wanted to arch into the touch. Like a cat. "Was that...?" I cleared my throat, surprised at how hoarse my voice had gotten. "What's the verdict?"

I tried to keep my voice light, but was sure I failed.

But Nathan's pupils were wide, revealing only a thin ring of that gorgeous blue, and he looked beautiful like this, flushed and breathing hard, and now I knew the noises he made when I touched him, and I was pretty sure I knew what the answer was going to be.

Hope, powerful enough to make me lightheaded, surged up my spine.

"That was amazing," he breathed. His eyes dropped to my mouth, then my chest, then lower, before rising up, a heated once-over that made me shiver and bite my lower lip, earning his gaze again. He gently touched my mouth with his thumb, pulling my lip free, and then dragged his thumb down my chin, the center of my throat, and flattened his hand on my chest. He could probably feel how hard my heart was racing.

"I think I could keep kissing you forever," he whispered, a breathless confession that felt more intimate than anything said in a church. His lips twitched. "Are you going to puke on me?"

I laughed. I had to, there was no other way to get all this energy out. "No, I think you're safe," I replied.

He smiled, and leaned in again, resting our foreheads together. He sighed. "Does that answer your question, then?" he asked. I liked how low his voice was, now, like it was coming from deep in his chest.

I swallowed, and nodded shallowly. I brushed my hands down his shoulders, gripping his biceps gently. "Pretty thoroughly. You're an excellent communicator," I teased. He grinned, and, like he just couldn't resist, kissed me again. He was good at that, too, and I clutched at his arms and arched against him, desperate for more.

"Randall!"

I jerked back, only saved from cracking my skull against the wall by Nathan's quick reflexes. He smiled at me, and I swallowed hard, hoping my voice didn't come out as fucked-out as I felt. "What is it, Mabel?"

"A new car just arrived. I think it might be Nathan's parents!"

"God damn it," I hissed, unable to help myself. Nathan laughed, and leaned in to kiss my cheek, and gave my chest a consoling pat.

"They always had the worst timing," he said, and pulled away. How the Hell he expected me to stay upright without help, I had no idea. I had to use the chair, and thought of dirty dishes and that one time I saw a piece of roadkill being eaten by crows on the side of the road to will away the arousal burning low in my stomach.

I sighed, rubbing a hand over my face. New guests meant more money, and I was in no position to turn that away, even when the alternative was making out with Nathan some more. And maybe other things. But I wasn't in any hurry to rush into that sort of thing. Nathan might have only been with women but the notches in my bedpost weren't even close to double digits either.

I looked mournfully down at our half-eaten eggs. We hadn't even gotten a chance to get to the biscuits and bacon, or touched the coffee. Nathan smiled, and squeezed my shoulder in reassurance. "I'll pack this up," he said. "I'll be out in a minute, promise."

I nodded and swallowed harshly. I flexed my fingers and ran my hands through my hair, hoping I didn't look as disheveled as I felt. I was sure the red on my cheeks was permanent at this point, and my mouth felt tender, but maybe that wouldn't look too out of the ordinary to someone who had never met me. If Mabel could keep her mouth shut, I'd be golden.

I sighed, and shook it off. "See you out there," I said. Nathan grinned at me, and his eyes raked me up and down one more time, dark with promise. Anticipation. Damn it.

Chapter Eight

Nathan

I was on cloud fucking nine. It felt like back in college when my roommate had convinced me to try weed for the first time. I had never made a habit of it, mostly because I immediately got sleepy and didn't get to appreciate the effects, but the half hour before that happened, I had felt so mellow, so good all over. The body high was indescribable.

I felt that way after kissing Randall.

I hadn't lied – I'd never really looked at men that way before. But I hadn't looked at women that way either. Sure, I could appreciate an attractive woman, but any that found me mutually attractive enough to approach, or not be put off when I approached them, usually lost interest once we started talking. Because I had a sense of humor that usually came off as dark and asshole-ish. Vicky had liked that, though. So had my college girlfriend, Olivia. Between them was a pattern of one-night stands and fleeting affairs.

Randall, though. He was the first person I just felt comfortable with. Maybe that was saying something. I liked being close to him. I liked making him laugh, and smile – he had a nice smile, all toothy and big like a little kid at Christmas.

And I admired the fact that he ran his own business, small and suffering though it was. The connection to family legacy and desire to keep something going that he felt was important to him was one I admired and resonated with deeply.

He was good-natured and conscientious, accommodating, a natural caretaker. Those were good things, and rare things to find, especially in a man. And I probably hadn't been a good emulator of that behavior in my own relationships in the past. Vicky's reservations about starting a family with me hadn't been unfounded.

But Randall made it all seem so easy. He put people at ease, and that was a damn diamond in the rough quality if I ever saw one.

I could hear my parents enter the bed and breakfast, even from the kitchen. They were loud people. My mother liked to comment on everything she saw, and my father was naturally boisterous, and was going deaf, which hadn't helped things.

I listened as they came in, ringing the little bell. Randall's answers and spiel were muted, but I knew when he was speaking, even if I didn't get the words clearly. His drawling accent was soft and soothing, and I found myself smiling when I heard it.

I couldn't remember feeling like this for anyone before. Maybe the first time my parents had brought Leah home, but even then, that had been a proud, brotherly love and attachment. Just hearing Randall talk, knowing he was in the next room, made me want to hurry up putting things away and be close to him again.

Maybe it was puppy love, maybe it was the start of some deeper and more powerful connection, but I'd never felt it before, and I wanted to feel it as much as I could.

I wrapped the bacon in foil and put it in the fridge. The eggs probably wouldn't keep well, so I threw them out, making a mental note to replace them. The biscuits would be fine, left out, so I covered them in Clingfilm and left them on the counter. The coffee would probably be fine in the carafe, too.

I washed my hands, and pushed through the door leading to the lobby.

"Nathan!" my mother cried immediately. She circled the desk and threw her arms around me. My mother barely crested my shoulders even when on her toes, but she was built like a bear, and when she wrapped her arms around my neck and hauled me down for a hug, there was no way to stop her. I stumbled awkwardly into a half-crouch and hugged her back. Over her shoulder, I could see Randall grinning, his eyes soft with affection as he watched us.

The card machine he was using beeped, and he took the card out and handed it back to my father. Retired Staff Sergeant Louis Monroe was a broad, barrel-chested man, with a thick mustache and head of thinning gray hair. He stood perfectly upright at all times, and had a stern gaze ever present beneath his bushy eyebrows.

"Thank you," he said primly, taking the card back along with his driver's license. My mother finally let me go, allowing me to straighten, and my father gave me a nod and shook my hand. "You're looking well, Nathan."

"Yes, Sir," I said. "How was your trip?"

"Without issue," he replied.

"We were caught in quite a storm last night," my mother said, looping her arm through mine and squeezing like a boa. She grinned up at me. "Leah tells me you had one here, too. I hope it clears up by this weekend!"

"The forecast is promising," my father said.

Randall cleared his throat, calling their attention. "Your room is 2A," he said. "The key is in the door. Do you need help with your bags?"

"No, thank you," my father replied sternly. It looked like he had packed lightly too, as I had. My mother's suitcase was another matter entirely. No wonder they hadn't flown. Despite his protests, I took my mother's bag, because that was the polite thing to do as the son. I looked over my shoulder to see Randall grinning, and carried the heavy bag upstairs – Jesus, did she pack rocks in this thing? – behind them.

"It's so good to see you, baby," my mother said, chattering and high pitched. "How are you? Are you doing okay? Still enjoying the city? What have you been up to lately? I..."

"Mom," I said, with a sigh and shake of my head. "Breathe." She rolled her eyes at me. "I'm fine. I'm doing fine. The city is great. I've been working and travelling, nothing out of the ordinary." I carried her bag to their room, noting that it was rather far away from my own, even between floors. "If you want, after you guys get settled in and maybe get some rest, I'll take you out to dinner and we can catch up."

"That would be lovely," she cooed, and yanked me into another tight hug. "I think that would be good. Wouldn't that be good, Louis? Before Leah gets here and we're all caught up in the wedding preparations." She laughed.

"Yes," my father said shortly, nodding.

"I'll leave you to it."

I left the room and hurried back downstairs, breathing a sigh of relief. Randall took one look at me and leaned against the front desk. He looked like he was trying very hard not to laugh. I arched a brow, approaching him, and smiled. "Something on your mind?"

"Your parents are..." He choked on the word, clamping a hand over his mouth. He drew in a calming breath. "They seem like very vibrant people."

I narrowed my eyes playfully. "This is when you say something like 'Bless their hearts', right?"

Randall gasped, offended. "I'm not an asshole," he teased.

"Mm, I don't know, I think you might be," I replied with a grin. He rolled his eyes. "I noticed you put them in a room quite far from mine. I appreciate that. Dad snores."

"Yeah, well." He cleared his throat, cheeks turning a very dark red. I tilted my head to one side, and he bit his lower lip, smiling nervously. "They're actually far away from... both of our rooms. In case there, ah, comes a situation where we might be making a lot of noise."

I blinked. Oh. "Oh," I breathed. Now that was an interesting concept.

Randall's cheeks were cherry red. I smiled, and moved so that my body was blocking any view from the door. Mabel had moved from her reading nook, presumably in her own room so that she didn't have to be around loud strangers. It was just us.

I hooked a finger beneath Randall's chin and made him rise. His eyes, already naturally dark, were almost all black in my shadow. "Do you want to make noise?" I asked.

Randall swallowed audibly. "Maybe," he said. "Do you...?"

I kissed him, gripping the back of his neck so he couldn't pull away. Not that he tried, not even a little. In fact, if the desk wasn't between us, he probably would have lunged for me right then and there. Tension changed how he moved, like a racehorse in the starting gate just ready to gallop.

When I pulled back for air, he was panting. His fingers curled into a fist at the front of my shirt. "Now who's the asshole?" he complained.

I laughed, and kissed his forehead. "I'll make it up to you later," I promised. Truthfully, with more confidence than I felt. I'd never been with a man, but being with Randall was comfortable, and made me feel confident. I couldn't imagine that would change in any setting. Patience and learning were required for any skill, and as long as we kept with the whole 'honesty' thing, then there was no reason to be nervous.

Not that it wasn't kind of satisfying to see him get all flustered.

Randall straightened, shaking his head so I had to let go of him. He was smiling, shy and eager. "Well, I need to start doing my shit," he told me, and I nodded. I should check in with my clients, too, and make sure there weren't going to be any more surprises like Leah showing up out of the blue with her entire entourage.

"I'm taking my parents to dinner," I told him. "Maybe I'll... see you after?"

"Yeah," Randall said. "Yeah. I'd like that."

Chapter Nine

Randall

Mabel returned as if waiting for her cue, as soon as I was finished cleaning hers and Nathan's room. It felt weird, being in the space of the man who had not even an hour ago pushed me up against the wall and kissed the living daylights out of me, but I was a professional, and it was just a room, in the end. Though I did have to judge him a little for his treatment of yesterday's clothes. Mabel was due for laundry anyway, so I added his outfit to mine and hers, and started a load in the giant washing machine in the back room, past the kitchen.

Then, I cleaned the breakfast dishes and wiped the kitchen down. Nathan had been pretty clean, all in all. I was impressed despite myself. Most bachelors I knew lived little better than animals, and maybe I would be one of them had I not literally been raised in a business that relied on keeping things clean.

Mabel was in her reading nook when I was done in the kitchen. "I'm doing your laundry," I told her. She nodded. "Do you want some tea?"

"I'm alright, dear, thank you." She closed her book and gave me a wide smile. Her eyes flashed, in the way those of a mother did when she caught her child hiding something behind his back. "You seem different."

I blushed. I couldn't help it. "What do you mean?"

"I think you know what I mean."

I sighed. It was useless hiding from her, anyway. "Nathan overheard us," I told her. "And apparently he's not as... strictly straight as either of us thought."

She laughed. "Well, I'm happy for you, dear."

I swallowed. "Did you... know?" I asked, shifting my weight nervously.

"Oh, I would never claim to know that sort of thing," she said coolly. "But I'm not surprised."

"Mm."

"Are you happy with this new development?" she asked, closing her book and meeting my gaze.

I smiled. "Yeah. I really am."

"Then that's all that matters, isn't it?" she replied, smiling as well. "Though I do worry. This isn't his home, and I don't think he would want to move. Are you going to leave?"

I frowned. "I mean..." ...No, of course I wouldn't. This bed and breakfast was my life, and had been in my family for decades. I liked Nathan, a lot, but I didn't want to live in the city, and packing up everything and moving halfway across the country just on the off chance of being with a guy I liked was way too risky. I wasn't a risk-taker, that wasn't in my blood.

But Nathan also traveled a lot, so if I lived in New York, or here, or Mexico, would it matter? He would still visit, would still be welcome here. "I... guess that's something I should talk about with him," I relented, sighing. "But I couldn't possibly abandon you."

She laughed, letting me lighten the mood with my bad joke. "Well, I'm sure you're both perfectly capable of finding a happy solution," she said, reaching out to gently pat my hand. "Every relationship is about compromise and dedication. You're a smart boy, and he seems to have a good head on him. Even if it doesn't work out, there's no reason you can't remain friends."

"Yeah," I said, nodding. It did make me feel better to realize that. To hope for that. "You're right."

"I always am," Mabel said with a winning smile.

Chapter Ten

Randall

I didn't get a chance to talk to Nathan all day. He ended up being on the phone and working with his clients, or with his parents. I wished them a good night when they went out to dinner, on Mabel's recommendation, for the pizzeria on the other side of town that was only kept alive by the fact that it was cheap enough for high schoolers.

Which left me alone. Mabel had gone to bed a while ago, with fresh clothes from the laundry. I had returned Nathan's clothes to him too, finding him in the middle of a conference call. He had smiled at me, apologetically, thanked me with a nod when I returned his outfit, and muted himself long enough for one chaste kiss before he had to get back to work.

Normally I would pass the time watching something on my computer until I got tired, but the recent conversation with Mabel occupied my thoughts. I really did need to talk to Nathan, and soon, just to calm my own anxieties. He had been honest with me about his work, and his travel. It had been the reason for his divorce. I had no reason to expect he would change anything about it.

And I didn't want him to. He clearly enjoyed his job, and it was important, I believed that. I just had to make sure he didn't think that I was going to pack up and move for his sake. I was smarter than that. Hell, if I thought leaving town and making a new life for myself somewhere else was in the cards, I would have done it already.

But this was my home. This one-horse town was where I belonged. Even though there was nothing in terms of prospects for a relationship, and money was scarce, I wasn't going to give any of it up. And I needed him to know that, so that neither of us got in too deep and ended up getting hurt.

The bell above the door rang, catching my attention. It opened, revealing a slim blonde, all legs. She looked like a swimmer, or a runway model, even with her hair in a loose bun and dressed in yoga pants and an oversized hoodie – which I assumed belonged to the man who followed her in. He was stocky and bearded, hair cut short on top in a military buzzcut.

"Evening!" she chirped. I recognized her voice from the phone.

I smiled at her. "You must be Leah," I said.

"Oh, my reputation precedes me," she giggled, approaching the desk, the man I assumed was her fiancé following her in. "That's me. Leah and Josh, checking in."

"It's nice to finally meet you," I said, as I fetched the sign-in sheet and the card machine. "Nathan's told me a lot about you."

"All terrible, I hope," she said with a wink. She signed her name with a flourish, and handed over her credit card without prompting. As I booted up the machine, she looked around, smiling widely. "God, this place is even prettier in person. Do you own it?"

"Yes, ma'am."

"It's gorgeous," she sighed. "Isn't it gorgeous, Josh?"

"Yeah," he replied. Not a man of many words, apparently.

The card machine finally finished waking up and I stuck her card in, waiting while it connected for the first transaction. "Nathan and your parents are at the pizzeria down the street," I told her while we waited. "They didn't leave all that long ago, if you wanted to join them."

"Oh, sweet! Thanks," she said. The transaction finished, coughing up the receipt, and I handed it back to her along with her I.D. card.

"You're in 2B," I said, and gestured to the stairs. "We serve breakfast at seven in the dining room." I pointed in the other direction, and she nodded attentively. "And if you want to go to the lodge tomorrow, I can have someone take you up there. The roads are kind of tricky, so I'd recommend having a local drive you up the first time."

"That would be great... Randall?" she hazarded. I nodded, and her smile widened. Clearly, she took more after her mother than Nathan did, in terms of demeanor. "Fantastic. Thank you! Have a good night!"

They took their bags upstairs, leaving me alone again. I didn't have Nathan's cell number, so I couldn't let him know that she had arrived, but doubted he would be left in the dark for long. Not even ten minutes later, they came back downstairs. Leah had changed into a pair of shorts, still with that giant hoodie, and pulled her hair up into a more proper ponytail. She laced her fingers with Josh's and they left the lobby with another wave over her shoulder.

I smiled, watching them go, and wished, for a moment, that I could go with them and see how Nathan behaved around all of his family. My mother used to say you could tell a lot about someone from how they interacted with the people who had raised them. Seeing Nathan with his father had certainly explained a lot, his stiff and proper nature, his adherence to the rules, his value of honesty and straightforwardness. As well, with his mother, her happy demeanor and welcoming attitude.

I sighed, and sat down at the reading nook, dimming the lights. The rest of the wedding party and guests would likely arrive tomorrow. It was going to be a busy day for both of us. Nathan had said we would hang out after dinner with his parents, but if he was too tired, I certainly wouldn't hold it against him.

I hoped, though. Seeing Nathan around his family and his sister's friends might bring me dangerously close to falling in love with the guy, and I'd rather know what the future might look like for us, before I let myself take that final step.

Chapter Eleven

Nathan

Seeing Leah at dinner was a surprise, but a welcome one. I hugged her tightly and asked her how her trip was, and immediately she and my mother began talking about the wedding plans and how everything was going to be organized. It was a relief for me, because it meant that the heat and focus was off me, and how I was doing, how I was handling the divorce, and everything else under the rainbow that I didn't want to talk about.

I clasped Josh's forearm in greeting, and he took a seat next to me. Leah was opposite him, by my mother, my father at the head of the table as he always was. It was like being back home with my family, except better in a way, because I knew when it was over, I was going to get to go back to the bed and breakfast. I wasn't going home to an empty apartment, or the pull-out futon in my parents' living room.

I was going to see Randall.

I'd always thought this kind of puppy love was ridiculous. I'd seen it in Leah so many times I'd lost count. Even Josh, as enamored as they had been with each other, didn't seem permanent. But here he was, two years later, about to marry my sister. To start a family with her, and give her everything she ever wanted.

I was happy for her, for both of them. And I had never been more grateful that they had chosen this middle of nowhere, forgettable town. I was going to have to get Leah a thousand presents to thank her for her ridiculous whims.

Thankfully, everyone was tired from travelling, so dinner didn't stretch on too long. I rode with Leah and Josh in their car back to the bed and breakfast, to spare myself any further questioning from my parents. I wished them all a good night as they ascended the stairs, but remained in the lobby.

Randall wasn't there, so I went searching for him. Through the kitchens, and into the laundry room. I searched the dining room, and then even went up to my own room to see if he had snuck in, even though he said the guest key was the only copy.

He wasn't there, though. I frowned, and went back downstairs to search. "Randall?" I called hesitantly. If he was asleep, I didn't want to wake him up. God knew how early he usually had to get up to prepare breakfast for everyone.

"In here," I heard him reply, from the second door behind the front desk. I followed the sound of his voice, down a short hallway that led to a miniature apartment suite. The living space was small, and cramped with a large couch taking up most of the space. Randall was on it, reading a book. He looked up and smiled at me as I entered, putting his book down as I closed the door. He sat forward. "Hey. How was dinner?"

"Good," I replied. "Tiring."

He nodded, and reached for me. I took his hand and let him pull me onto the couch, until we sat side by side. I put my hand on his thigh, and felt him thrumming with tension. The good kind, I hoped.

He scratched the back of his neck and sighed, meeting my eyes. "I wanted to talk to you about something," he said. I nodded, unable to stop the little fissure of anxiety that curled in the back of my skull. He looked down, biting hard on his lower lip. I felt compelled to reach up and tug it free, and he met my eyes again.

"What's... the plan, here?" he asked, and winced at his own wording. "I mean. I know you live in New York. That you like it there. But I live here. I know you travel, and I don't. Like, I'm not like your ex-wife. I don't expect you to just stay here all the time or anything like that, but I need you to know that this place is my home, and I'm not going to leave it."

Oh. I smiled, and nodded. "I didn't expect you to," I said. He blinked at me, clearly surprised. "And you know, I'll still travel. Still keep my place in New York. You can come visit if you ever want to, but you don't have to." I squeezed his thigh gently, and he shivered in answer. "I like you just the way you are, Randall. I wouldn't want to change anything about you."

His smile went wide, crinkling the corners of his eyes. "Okay," he breathed, the word thick with relief. "I just... Sorry." He laughed sheepishly. "Mabel mentioned it and I suddenly realized we hadn't actually... talked about this with any degree of permanency and, well, I needed to know if it was something you had even thought about, but then..."

"I understand," I said. He nodded again, with another shaky, relieved exhale. "And yes, I did. Like I said, I'm not used to this kind of thing with another man, but I don't think you being a guy would change how I feel about you, no matter what."

The pink on his cheeks was lovely. I had to kiss him, then. He met me eagerly, with a soft little sigh and a frantic arch into my hands. I pulled him into my lap, moaning roughly when he immediately settled across my thighs, his own clinging tightly, knees digging into the back of the couch. It was a deep-seated piece of furniture, and I didn't have to worry about him falling off.

His hands curled in my hair, tugging hard enough to make me gasp, a fierce shot of pleasure crawling right down my spine. He was so warm, and he had showered again. I was used to perfumes and fragrant shampoos, floral or fruity. But he just smelled of the outdoors, the forest, and grass, and the cedar oil he must have used to spray for bugs.

I wrapped my arms around his hips, pulling him closer, seeking friction as he kissed me. He was more confident this time, and sighed so quietly, so satisfied. It made me want to do anything I could to get him to make more noise. I liked it when my partners were vocal in bed, when they showed me what they liked. I wanted to learn him, every inch of him, with my hands and my mouth. I wanted to know how to make his pupils go big and his hands shake.

He pulled back, gasping for air, lashes low over his dark eyes, his cheeks red and mouth bruised. "God," he breathed, throat flexing as he swallowed, his hips jerking forward, rutting against me. He was hard, and the feeling of it, the obvious sign of how affected he was, hit me like another lungful of weed smoke. I was getting high off him.

I reached between us with one hand, flattening a palm against his erection. He stiffened, and let out an absolutely filthy sound, grinding against my hand. I smiled, and he smiled back, and dove in for another kiss, nails scratching over my scalp.

I wanted to touch him. I needed it.

"Can I...?" I dragged my fingers up, to the button of his jeans, waiting for permission.

"Please," he said, kissing the corner of my mouth, my jaw, down my neck as I took him out. The feeling of five o'clock shadow against my face was new, but nice. It made my skin sensitive, a burn that only added to the heat in my stomach. I unbuttoned and unzipped his jeans, and wormed my hand into the hole in the front of his underwear. He was so warm, leaking at the tip already, as I pulled him out and gave him a slow stroke.

He shuddered above me, another filthy noise growled right into my ear. Fuck, that was hot. I needed, suddenly, to know just what other noises I could pull from him. I wanted him to be loud. I wanted the whole damn town to hear how good I made him feel.

"Nathan," he sighed, hands dragging down to dig into my shoulders. It hurt. He could grip harder than a woman. He was strong, muscled, heavy on my lap. I wrapped my free hand around the back of his neck and kissed his racing pulse as I continued to stroke him. "I want you so fuckin' bad."

"How do you want me?" I breathed. At this point I didn't think there was anything I wouldn't let him do. "Whatever you want, Randall, I swear."

"God, don't say things like that," he said, with a breathless laugh. "You should know better, city boy."

I laughed. "But I mean it."

He pulled back, panting, no original color left in his eyes. He bit his lower lip and I had to lean forward and free it with my own teeth, coaxing him into another kiss. It was getting unbearably warm in Randall's living room, and the scent of his sweat, the taste of it on his neck, was new and fantastic and I wanted more of it.

"Just... Let me..." He pushed back, and sank to his knees on the floor in front of the couch. I watched him, wide-eyed, as he unfastened my jeans. I lifted my hips to help him pull my clothes down until they bunched around my knees.

He rose up, and I leaned in to kiss him again, right after he licked his palm and wrapped his slick fingers around my cock. He didn't hesitate even a little, thumb rubbing gently over the slit, beneath the head. It was like he had a map to every sensitive part of me. Every time I shivered, or gasped, or clenched my jaw, his eyes flashed with victory.

"Come here," he demanded, pulling me closer to the edge of the couch. He shoved my clothes down to my ankles so I had room to spread my knees, and shouldered his way between them. I could only grab his hair with a white-knuckled grip as he parted his lips and took me into his mouth.

Soaking wet, tight heat surrounded me. His red cheeks hollowed as he sucked, tongue curling around the tip as he closed his eyes, still stroking what he wasn't fitting in his mouth. I groaned, loudly, head tipped back as he sank down further. The muscles in his throat clenched around me, squeezing like the inside of a person, but he didn't stop.

"Oh my God, fuck, Randall," I gasped, when his nose pressed flush to me, when he had taken all of it. I tentatively felt along the front of his throat, and I could admit the sound I let out when I felt how his throat was so tense was closer to a whimper than anything else.

He pulled back with a gasp, sucking in a breath through his nose when he only had the tip in his mouth again, and tilted his head to meet my eyes. His own were wicked, smug, and God, I would happily have him look like that the rest of my life. The way his lips stretched around me was obscene, bruised and turning an even deeper red.

Then, he let go with his hands, flattened them on my thighs to pin me down, and started a rhythm. It was slow and torturous and absolutely perfect, even as I felt myself lose all coherent thought. There was nothing but his name, his mouth, his hands. His hair between my fingers. I did nothing to guide him, I wanted him to do this how he wanted. And this confidence, him taking charge, was even better than his flustered, nervous shyness.

I could only watch him, as he took me down again and again and again. He slid his hands up, cupping my ass, and I moaned weakly, obeying the unspoken order to thrust up into his mouth. He took it with another filthy, wet noise, eyes closed. He looked blissful.

"I'm..." I tried to warn him. All he did was hold on tighter and suck harder. My head fell against the back of the couch. My stomach tensed so hard it was almost painful, my thighs shaking, heart trying to beat its way out of my chest. "God, fuck, I..."

That was the only thing I could manage, before my orgasm hit me like a Goddamn train. He shoved himself down hard on me, taking it all, throat clenching with instinctive swallows as I spilled down it. Vicky had never let me do that. None of the women I'd slept with had let me do that. But Randall took it all, sucking lightly as I came. He pulled off slowly, once I'd finished, lips forming a tight seal. He let me go, and swallowed, and gasped.

Then, he grinned, smug as a well-fed cat that had caught its mouse. I lunged for him, gripping his hair with both hands, kissing him desperately. There was no coordination and I could feel how warm and sore his jaw and neck were, and taste myself on his tongue.

"Let me do something for you," I begged. "Please, Randall."

He grinned, lips swollen. He wiped his mouth with the back of his hand, and pushed me back on the couch, crawling over my shaking thighs. He settled there like he owned that spot, and fuck, maybe he did.

He wrapped a hand in my hair and tugged me back, until I arched up against him, pawing at his sides, his back, his hips. His free hand wrapped around his own cock, stroking quickly. From the heaviness of his breathing and the way he kept twitching, every inch of him, I guessed he was close too.

"Randall..."

"Shh," he purred, kissing me, again and again, and down my neck. He pulled back and tugged at my shirt and I yanked it over my head, throwing it to the floor behind me. His eyes raked me up and down in appreciation, smile wide, before he went right back to pulling on my hair. He shifted closer, so he could grind the tip of his leaking cock against my stomach. "Just like that, Nathan. Fuck, that was so hot. You're so vocal, I love it."

I clenched my jaw, letting him turn my head so he could bite, lightly, below my ear. I tensed up and shivered, surprised at how sensitive I was there. I pressed my hands to his chest, curling my fingers like it was all I could do to hold on.

He made another rough, filthy sound, and bit down on my shoulder, low enough a shirt would hide it, as he stroked himself and came on my chest and stomach. It was warm and wet, dirty and possessive. The sound of his satisfied moan made my spent cock twitch almost painfully.

Then, he sighed, and kissed over the mark he'd left, laughing quietly. He let go of his cock and wiped his hand on his own shirt, then took it off completely so he could clean me up. I could only stare at him, his mussed hair, red cheeks, mouth bruised to all Hell. It was one of the most primally satisfying things I'd seen in my entire life.

When I was passably clean, he tossed his shirt away. I only bothered with pulling my underwear back up, kicking off my shoes and jeans, as he did the same, and we fell in a spent sprawl on the couch together, side by side because the couch was so deep.

I turned and rested my head on his shoulder, and smiled when he turned his head to look at me. "Well," I said lightly. "That's certainly going to leave a good impression."

He blinked at me, and then laughed, full-bellied and loud, and wiped a hand over his face. It was the hand he came in, I noticed, though he didn't seem to care. He pushed his hair out of his face, and then mine, tucking it behind my ear.

"I'll leave you with a thousand good impressions, time permitting," he teased.

I grinned. "Where did the shy little innkeeper go?" I asked.

"Oh, he's still here," Randall replied, and kissed my forehead. "But the horny side won out for a minute."

I laughed. "No complaints here."

He turned onto his side, so that he could more firmly wrap himself around me. We were both sweaty and it was far too hot, but I didn't mind. I liked the way he tucked his face against my neck, how solid and warm he felt. I liked tracing the muscles in his back with my hands as, piece by piece, every part of him went lax.

Chapter Twelve

Nathan

Leah's wedding went off without a hitch. The sky was cloudless, the air was warmed by the sun. She looked like a princess, her dress glistening with brilliant stones around her shoulders and waist, her lace train catching the light as she walked down the 'aisle' created by the two sets of chairs on the lawn. I wasn't part of the groom party, and I wasn't a bridesmaid, but I sat in the front row next to my mother and father, after he gave her away to Josh. It was the first time I'd ever seen tears in his eyes.

Randall showed her and Josh the little cove at the summit of the mountain afterwards. I went with them, because I wanted to be with them all – the two people I adored most, and now the newest member of our family. Leah was enthralled by the beauty of the place.

"Isn't it just like Heaven, Nathan?" she asked.

"It is," I couldn't help but agree, even though my eyes were on Randall when I said it.

When we all returned to the lodge, Leah changed into a dress that she could be comfortable in, and everyone started drinking and toasting and there was enough food to feed an army. I made sure I was sober enough to drive back. I had no intention of staying the night here. At best it would be a loud, drunken chorus of braying and jokes and Josh's friends making a nuisance of themselves. At worst, I'd overhear my sister on her wedding night, and that wasn't a situation any of us wanted to be in.

I ended up driving my parents back to the bed and breakfast while Leah, Josh, and their friends stayed to party at the lodge. I didn't care – they were loud and most of them were aggravating after a while, at least to me, and I made sure they knew Randall was fully in his rights to charge them for their unused rooms.

I bid my parents goodnight, and waited up for Randall. He had stayed behind with Darren to start cleaning up, so he could be out all night. I sighed to myself. I had a very early flight, so early that, realistically, I needed to call a taxi soon if I had a hope of making it to the airport in time.

I packed up my things. My parents didn't like that I was leaving so soon, but my clients wouldn't wait forever, and though I had plenty of vacation time built up, my company cashed it out at the end of the year, so it was just money in the bank if it went unused. I wasn't hurting for money, absolutely not, but I was going to be taking a lot more trips in my future to this little town in the middle of nowhere, and it was always good to have a cushion.

Randall ended up rolling in just past midnight. My taxi was ten minutes away. I regretted taking that flight, now, but I had meetings scheduled the next morning and so I couldn't reasonably delay or extend my trip. This was the first time, in a long time, I had a person worth cancelling a trip for.

He smiled at me when he entered, but his eyes quickly took in my bag, and darkened with sadness. He sighed. "Soon?"

"Fifteen minutes, tops," I told him.

He nodded, and approached me. We had spent every night together since the first one, though not nearly enough, in my opinion. I didn't want to leave him. I didn't want to go back to my empty apartment in a city that never shut up for two damn seconds. I didn't want garish fluorescent lights in my office, where everything was black and chrome, and people who wore four figure suits were blaming me for their own oversights when it came to employees stealing funds.

I didn't particularly want to stay here, though, either. Highland Falls was nice, but it was small, and there wasn't much to do.

Randall cupped my face and kissed me, drawing me out of my thoughts. "Don't leave me just yet," he teased. His eyes were still sad, but I could tell he was trying not to be, for my sake.

I sighed, resting our foreheads together. "I'm here," I said.

His smile widened. He kissed me again, and coaxed me to the reading nook, so we could sit side by side and look out the window to see when my taxi got here. He laced his fingers with mine and pressed his lips together.

"You know," he said idly. "After the wedding party leaves, I don't think I'll have much in the way of guests for a while."

I turned to him. "Mabel?"

"She can take care of herself for a few days," Randall said, smiling. "She already told me that she'd, I think she specifically used the words 'Tan your hide darker than the pit of Hell', if I didn't get over myself and come visit you."

I laughed. Honestly, God bless little old lady busybodies. "You don't have to," I said, like I promised last time. "But if you want to, I'm sure I could give you some good impressions of New York."

Randall smiled. "I'd like that," he replied, quietly. He met my eyes, and kissed my cheek, first. Then the corner of my jaw. Then my neck, over the collar of my shirt. Below it, there was a dark bruise in the shape of his mouth that throbbed tenderly under the pressure, or whenever I moved just right. It matched the lines I had clawed into Randall's back, and the bruises he sucked onto my thighs and my chest, and the bite mark I'd left on his hipbone.

"Promise me you'll call me when you land," he said. "No matter what time it is."

"I will," I replied. It would probably be the first thing I did, as soon as I could turn off airplane mode. Even now, my cell phone felt like it was burning a hole in my pocket.

A flash of lights from the outside caught my attention. Randall sighed, and squeezed my hand, before getting up to let me out of the little nook. I couldn't help but cup his face and kiss him one more time – deeply, just to hear him gasp, and feel him shiver against me. It already felt like I hadn't touched him in years, and I felt every second with a deep, deep ache in my chest.

I went out and got into the taxi. He didn't seem to like the idea of driving all the way to Chattanooga airport, but even the most reluctant of drivers could be enticed with some extra cash. I turned around to watch the bed and breakfast until it disappeared. Randall's silhouette in the window felt like a beacon, calling me back.

The drive was long, but the flight was mercifully short. I ended up landing in J.F.K. at seven in the morning, and felt exhausted.

But I called him. Of course I did.

"Hey," he breathed. He sounded tired too, like he had been waiting up all night for me. But, for him, it was six in the morning, so he would have been awake at this time anyway.

"Hey," I replied, unable to hide the affection in my voice. Not that I wanted to. I didn't need to hide anything from him. "Just landed. About to get off the plane."

"No trouble?" he asked.

"None," I said. "How was your night?"

"Good," he replied. "Tiring. I, ah, had some trouble sleeping."

I sighed. "Yeah," I admitted. "I don't think I'll be good company at the office today."

"You're going in today?" Randall said, incredulously.

I laughed. "No rest for the wicked," I replied with a shrug. "Or the people who hunt them."

"Well. Be safe," he said quietly. "And promise me you'll get some rest."

"I will. Have a good day."

"Yeah, you too."

I hung up, just as the fasten seatbelt sign turned off, and rose to join the line of people trying to exit the plane. I had mastered the art of taking only one carryon, to avoid wrestling with overhead bins or baggage claim.

A company car was waiting to take me to the office. When I entered, Jimmy looked more relieved than if he'd just gotten negative results on a blood test. "You're back!" he said. I sighed inwardly, and nodded, as he rushed up to me with a stack of files. Jimmy was a good kid, if a little too energetic for his own good. "The Sanders account sent over their latest monthly report, and we have a new client who the boss wants you to take a look at. Also, did you already send over the briefing to the Townsend people? They're asking, and I could have sworn you sent it, but I can't find it anywhere and..."

"I'll handle it," I said, shaking my head. "Thank you, Jimmy." He nodded, and scurried away. I walked to my office and sat down, sighing inwardly. Everything was clean and neat and modern. No moldings on the doorways. No dark green, forest patterned carpet. There wasn't a single piece of wood in sight; the walls were plaster, the desks made of metal.

Though, honestly, I wasn't sure I missed any of those aesthetics, as much as the man they reminded me of. I wondered how long I could get away with making a 'work call' before someone noticed.

Probably not very long at all. And Randall had work to do, too. He had to check out Leah, Josh, and all their entourage, and then clean everything and get things back to normal. He still had a truck that needed repairs, and a business to keep afloat. Clingy behavior wasn't something either of us expected or demanded, and I could handle not talking to him for at least a solid work day.

The longer the day went on, the more on edge I became. I knew I was showing signs of it, too, and excused it to my coworkers and boss as exhaustion. I was allowed to go home early, but refused to take them up on the offer. I didn't want to go to my empty apartment, even if it meant being able to call Randall. It would just make me remember how far away he was.

But the day had to end eventually. I straightened out Sanders and Townsend, and took the new client's briefing home with me to work on, in the hope that it would keep me distracted enough.

I lived on one of the top floors of my apartment complex. The outside of the building was old and had been built during the industrial revolution, and had an old gothic aesthetic that usually, I hated. But I didn't hate it so much now, looking at it. The old building reminded me of Randall's bed and breakfast.

I went inside, across the too-white floors and towards the elevator, and rode it up. My apartment was down the hall and around the corner, and I took my time with each stride, dreading the point where I would get in. It was times like this when I did regret not having a larger friend group, but that wasn't something I could fix now.

I rounded the corner, and stopped dead in my tracks.

"Randall?" I breathed.

He looked up, smiling widely at me. He was sitting on the floor with his back to my door, a giant duffel bag by his side. He stood as I approached, and I was sure it was the fastest I'd ever moved. I hauled him into my arms in a way I'm sure was just like my mother, and he collapsed against me with a soft 'oof', but laughed, hugging me back just as tightly.

"How did you -?"

"Leah left a very generous tip," he said, pulling back, grinning. "And Mabel paid for a month in advance, and Darren split the lodge rental with me as thanks for helping to clean up and everything. So I had some money leftover, and flights aren't that expensive."

"The drive to the airport, though?" I asked.

"Your parents drove me," he said, blushing lightly. "I think they like me."

I blinked at him, surprised. "Do they... know?" I asked.

"Your mother has some startlingly good intuition," he said, shrugging. "I didn't want to lie to her."

Well. That was... Something.

"Is that...? I'm sorry, I know this is a new thing for you but I just didn't want to lie to her face and..."

"Stop fucking apologizing," I said, throwing his own words back at him. He laughed, and I had to kiss him. I had to. The door groaned in warning when I shoved him against it, and it had been barely a day and a half since I'd seen him, but it felt like too long.

"How long are you staying for?" I asked into his mouth.

"Until I don't feel like I'm going to die when you're not kissing me," he replied, laughing. I smiled with him. "But more like two weeks. So we don't do something stupid and mess this up."

"We're not going to mess it up," I promised. I had never been so sure of anything in my life.

Randall's eyes shone with affection, that beautiful pink stain back on his cheeks. He bit his lower lip and I tugged it free, and he rolled his eyes, and gestured behind him to the door. "So," he said, lashes low, "you gonna let me in or what?"

I grinned, and kissed him one more time, until I felt him go lax. Then, I pulled away, grabbed and shouldered his bag, and opened the apartment. He followed me in, and closed and locked the door behind us.

I set his bag down, along with my own, and the new client file. He nodded to it. "Still have work to do?"

"No," I told him, and pulled him along to the couch. "You're more important."

"No complaints here," he replied, with a laugh that made me pull him close, and kiss him, and touch him, until the neighbors were sure to complain about the noise we both made, later.

*****

Don't miss out!

Visit the website below and you can sign up to receive emails whenever Van Cole publishes a new book. There's no charge and no obligation.

https://books2read.com/r/B-A-RTRV-FNHDC

BOOKS 2 READ

Connecting independent readers to independent writers.

Also by Van Cole

3 Man Huddle: MMM Best Friend Romance
His Alpha Wolf: Gay First Time Romance
A Dragon's Miracle: Gay Dragon MPREG Romance
Double-Teamed: MMM First Time Football Romance
His Football Star: Gay Second Chance Romance
Love In My Town: MM First Time Romance
Training A Hockey Star
Game Night
Double Shift
Take A Shot
Dear Professor
Getting Inked
Ninth Inning
Triple Threat
Seducing My Best Friend's Brother
My Protector
The Blueprint
Show Me The Way
End Zone
Matched To His Tiger
Love At First Puck
My Straight Boss
Falling For The Alpha
My Boss
On Thin Ice